Too Old, Too Fast

C. E. Andrews

Eloquent Books

Eloquent Books
An imprint of Strategic Book Group
P.O. Box 333
Durham CT 06422
www.StrategicBookGroup.com

ISBN: 978-1-60911-251-6

Printed in the United States of America

Book Design/Layout by: Andrew Herzog

Dedicated

To my dad and grandmother (Nanny): though both are gone, their lives inspired this book.

To my mom: for her dedication to my brother and me.

To the Lewis family: Chet, Lillian, Patty, Judy, and Jeannie. Thank you for the years of friendship.

While Chet is gone, we still have his memories with us.

I want to dedicate this book to Frankie Lewis, Chet and Lillian's only son, who lost his life in a car accident on New Year's Eve 1972, as a senior in high school.

Acknowledgements

This book would not have been possible without the care and love shown by so many.

First, I want to thank God for all He has done for me in my life and how He inspired the writing of this book.

Next, I would like to thank my wife for her patience, encouragement, love, and hard work in getting this book accomplished. I am truly blessed to have such a godly wife. I look forward to our remaining years together.

There are numerous others to thank: Gary and Mae Stiff for being such wonderful godly friends and for Gary's endless hours of encouragement, ideas, and corrections. Gary is the closest thing to a co-author I know; without him this work would never have been completed. Sandy Williams, thanks for reading through the rough draft and encouraging me to finish it. You are a dear friend to Deb and me, may our Lord richly bless you.

A special thank you to author David Deranian, who got me started in the story and helped me organize my thoughts.

Contents

Introduction

Welcome to the late 1920s and 1930s. Follow the struggles of a family and the people who surround them as they face adverse situations common to the time. They're a typical family like so many today, just transplanted eighty years back. You'll read about things that will be hard to comprehend in the present day, but was reality to all too many back then.

Although a fictional book, it's filled with historical facts about the times. The story line's based from my dad's formidable years. So many things happening around these times: Prohibition, The Depression, and The Dust Bowl to name a few. This is our country's history that we must never lose and the people who lived through it must never be forgotten.

No matter what period of time, whether back seventy or eighty years ago or today, we must all live with our decisions. Watch this become reality for so many of the characters. I pray you enjoy the book.

> Situations cause dilemmas
> Dilemmas cause decisions
> Decisions cause results
> Results cause situations
> —C. E. Andrews

Chapter 1

The Family

One Sunday afternoon the family gathers for a barbeque. My sons and I are sitting in the family room with the background sounds of grandkids and a ballgame on TV. It's great to hear the sounds of little ones running through the house again. One makes a sudden stop by the bookshelf, looks up, and asks, "Papa, is that a real cowboy hat and horseshoe? Can I play with it?"

His dad looks over at him and says, "No, son. There's a story behind that; right Pop?"

Rising from the chair, I take the old hat and horseshoe from the shelf and place the hat on my head. Picking up my grandson and sitting back down in my rocker, I reply, "Yeah, there is!" My mind swirls with the story as my son asks, "Pop, why don't you tell us about it?"

That's all the encouragement I need. "Don't believe I've ever told you the story of our family." Everyone gathers around and the grandkids lay on their bellies at my feet, eagerly anticipating what comes next. The adults sit in silence, and someone reaches over and turns off the TV. All eyes are on me as I begin.

It's early morning; the sun peeks through the clouds over the eastern plain in this southern central valley of Colorado, better known as the San Luis Valley. It runs approximately 122 miles long and 74 miles wide, and extends from the Continental Divide on the northwest rim into New Mexico on the south, with an average elevation of 7,500 feet.

In a small ranch house in this Colorado valley, the Lewis family begins to stir. Mom, Dad, and four kids have lived here most of their lives. They're a close-knit family that enjoys each other's company and looks out after each other. Like any other family, they have their squabbles and disagreements, but they do all they can to maintain unity within the family.

As usual, Mom, or Dorris, her given name, busily prepares breakfast on the potbellied stove that stands in the middle of the room. With her flowered apron, she wipes the sweat from her brow caused by the radiant heat of the stove. Mom loves her family and gives them her best, so when she isn't cooking, she's sewing clothes for the family or for extra money. Mom's a pretty little lady, small in stature but huge in commitment. Don't let her looks fool you though; she can stand her own with the best of them. While hard-working, she'd never use that as an excuse for not looking her best for her man and her family. You'll always find her dressing in beautiful Victorian-style dresses which, by the way, she's sewn; she loves the looks she gets from her man.

Living here on the ranch is totally different from how she was raised. She grew up in a well-to-do family in Indiana with few worries. Her dad was a successful businessman, well-known throughout the community. Everywhere they went, people knew them. She hated it. Her family had a rich heritage; Grandpa had fought in the Civil War and was wounded twice, the last one so severely he could hardly get around on his own. People always told her she was a lot like him, a no-nonsense type of person, not looking for any handouts. Her life embodies doing what you commit to, no matter what. She remembers her grandpa's favorite saying, "Work out your worries." It had become Mom's motto, too. She doesn't need to impress anyone. Country living is the life for her; the farther away from people, the better.

Dad, or Elmer, on the other hand, is foreman for the Livingstons on their 12,800-acre ranch. It's a tough job—sometimes seven days a week, from dawn till dusk. He started working for them just after Ruthie, their fourteen-year-old daughter, was born. Elmer grew up a wanderer, never really knowing his family or parents. When pressed, he really couldn't tell you anything about either parent. He wandered from meal-to-meal in a small town in Eastern Kansas. Not the best-looking of men, but having the work ethic of a plow horse, he stood about 6 feet 1, with an olive complexion. The more sun he got, the darker he became. Ranch work keeps him in great shape. He is well-built and strong as an ox with big hands that squeeze like a vise, and he's always with a Ten-Gallon Stetson and his favorite black duster coat.

Numerous rumors float around as to how they came up with the term *Ten-Gallon Hat*. The most common one had to do with them being waterproof, and they're almost indestructible. Densely felted wool, they were strong enough to be used as a bucket to draw water with or to give your horse a drink. Dad's hat began as silver-gray with a four-inch crown and brim and a small leather headband. The brim is curled on the sides, so much in fact, that the tips almost touch the crown. Dad used his duster coat to guard his clothing from trail dust, sliced up the back to the hip to make it easier to wear while riding his horse or in the motorcar.

Elmer loves his Dorris, and their four children are the "apples of his eye." His desire is to give them the best life he can, which he diligently works to fulfill for them. While loving all his kids and spending time with each one is important, Clyde, his only son, is the closest to his heart. He recalls this kind of love found in the Scriptures with Jacob and Joseph. While he doesn't want to be as extreme with his love as Jacob, he can understand how it can happen, so he's always very careful.

Clyde loves spending every available moment with Dad. He's a quick learner and eager to get his hands dirty. Dad teaches Clyde all he can, but the things they love doing together are fishing and hunting. Of the two, fishing is Clyde's favorite. He explains it this way, "Ya see fishin', ya can talk, but huntin', ya need to be quiet." Being quiet goes against his grain, because he enjoys talking—especially with Dad. He's his hero, and he'll do anything he can to make him proud.

The Livingstons, Walter and Maggie, owners of the ranch for some twenty-five years, grew up in Kansas and this ranch was their dream. They were friends long before they married. Their two families lived next to each other in Plains, Kansas, and were best friends until they argued over religion. Walter and Maggie, born the same year, with Walter only six months older, never understood how their parents could allow something like this to destroy a friendship. The battle got so bad that the parents banned them from seeing each other. They continued to, however. The way they looked at it, this was a battle between the parents and had nothing to do with them. They knew they were made for each other, and God confirmed that in various ways; however, neither set of parents would listen. With that, they made plans and without their parents' permission, Walter and Maggie decided to marry, thinking this would help heal things. It only got worse, and when they couldn't take the tension any longer, they headed to California.

On their way, they came across this beautiful valley and couldn't imagine anything better. As life would have it, they began to settle in, and over the years continued to purchase land until they had this beautiful ranch. Everything seemed to fall into place. Some say it was pure luck how they came upon this good-sized ranch, but Walter would always say that it was God's special blessing. You see, he and Maggie were unable to have children, so their "baby" was the ranch and they pampered it, took care of it with such a love of thankfulness that few people understood. They got to know Elmer and Dorris when Elmer came looking for a job. Their cute little daughter had just been born, and the Livingstons couldn't say no. Through the years they became like family, and the Livingstons look at the Lewis' kids as the grandkids they could never have. They were truly their family.

On this brisk morning, Elmer is outside saddling the horse that will be his transportation for the next two, maybe three days. He's headed out to check the fence line around this 20-square-mile ranch. The breeze is steady and the air is brisk these early morning hours, so Elmer continually slaps his hands across his trousers to keep them warm. As he throws the saddle blanket over the back of his horse, Sacred, he is reminded how special this blanket is. Dorris pieced it together as a special gift to him for their anniversary. It's approximately 35-inches square and twice as thick as the store-bought ones. The multicolored blanket is a kaleidoscope of earth tones that serves multiple purposes. Placed under the saddle, it is a cushion that helps protect the horse's back, and it absorbs his sweat.

Standing 14.5 hands or 58 inches tall, Dad's horse, Sacred, is a beautiful white Pinto, with blotches of black on the hind quarters and a black facemask. Even though there had been some evidence of these horses being brought to the Americas by the South American Conquistadors, most of them were shipped from Europe. They were popular in the Seventeenth century in Europe, and Dad loves this horse. While having others to choose from, Sacred is Dad's favorite. He always accompanies him on these types of working trips. One of the main reasons is that from past experiences, Dad knows that if something were to go wrong, he can count on Sacred.

He finishes saddling Sacred, along with his early morning chores, and places his hands under his armpits to try to keep them warm. He thinks back to his last trip. It was toward the end of the first day, 'bout dusk, after a long, hard ride and a full day of hard labor. After searching and finding a watering hole, he squatted to fill his canteens. As he began filling the second one, he was startled by a growling sound coming from behind. He turned to his left as a mountain lion began its charge. He froze, not knowing what to do next. This big cat was picking up speed and in a matter of seconds would pounce on him. He fell to the ground, covering himself the best he could. Then from his right peripheral vision, he noticed something moving. First, he thought it was another cat, but just before the cat leaped, this wonderful, beautiful horse came to his rescue. He stepped between Elmer and the cat, rose up on his hind legs, and then stomped the ground with his front hooves. The cat had no choice but to turn its attention to Sacred; he was no match for this giant beauty. Taking a hard right, the mountain lion ran as fast as it could in the opposite direction, giving Elmer enough time to grab his rifle and fire off a couple of rounds in his direction. Sacred saved the day. Had it not been for Sacred, the Lord only knows what would have happened.

Dad shakes his head so as to shake the thoughts out, which brings him back to the reality of the moment, and thinks, *Something always seems to come up with each journey*, as he turns to walk back to the house. About halfway there, Clyde comes busting out of the house hollering, "Dad, take me with you; I want to go!" Clyde, always full of energy and in the mood for a new adventure, (a quality that would prove useful in coming years), reaches Dad with a big leap.

Elmer grabs him in midair and swings him around, setting him down after the first spin. As Clyde lands on his feet, he looks up at Dad, eagerly anticipating his response. Elmer kneels down, and with his index finger, tips his Stetson back. He looks into Clyde's deep blue eyes, sees his desire and love of just wanting to be with him, and replies in a soft voice, "Not this time, Clyde; maybe next time."

With disappointment in his eyes, Clyde replies, "Ah shucks, that's what you always say!" Clyde puts his head down, looks at the ground, and kicks up dirt clouds with his feet. Elmer, seeing his disappointment, immediately begins contemplating the possibility of him going along. Clyde can see that he has Dad on the ropes and goes in for the knockout. "Remember last time, ya said I could go next time? Well this is next time! Come on, Dad, please, please. Ya said it! Don't ya remember?"

Kneeling there, Elmer remembers saying that to Clyde, but he also realizes this is not the ride for him to go on. He quickly comes back, "I know, but this is not the right time. Instead of two days, I may be gone longer." Before Clyde has time to respond, Dad pulls his hat brim down to his eyebrows. Pulling Clyde close, in his raspy voice he says, "Let's make plans for an overnight stay when I get back—ya know, fishin' and huntin'!"

Clyde's eyes light up. He gives a big smile and whispers, "Should we tell Mom or keep it our secret?"

"Let's keep it between us men right now, but you plan the trip," Dad whispers back.

With that, Clyde gives Dad a big hug and inhales the comforting smell of the worn leather from Dad's hatband and coat collar. He would have hugged harder, but Dad's whiskers poked his tender, smooth cheeks pretty hard. Clyde lets go of Dad and takes off running, hollering as he runs, "I'll start right now."

Dad stands up and yells, "Don't forget your chores before school!"

He follows Clyde to the cottage door and walks up on the porch. He spits on the palm of his right hand, and passing through the doorway, slaps the worn, shiny horseshoe hung over the top doorpost. This is something Dad has done for many years. He had hung that old horseshoe up there for good luck, and it seemed to be working. It's been around longer than most of the kids.

As the door opens, the cool breeze rushes in. Mom, standing by the stove, gives a sigh of approval, "That feels pretty good to me."

Dad's ready for a warm-up. His hands are pretty chilly, so he walks over to the old stove, rubs them together, and places them about a foot above the stove. "Ah," he sighs, "that feels sooo good." Once warm, he turns around and walks over to the table on the far side of the room. Mom pours him a hot cup of coffee, being careful not to pour out the eggshell holding down the grinds, and sets his breakfast plate in front of him.

Dorris' breakfasts were always the best, usually biscuits and gravy, Dad's favorite. The kids hurry to get their chores done before heading off to school. As they wrap up their final chores, they each give Dad a squeeze and kiss before starting their long walk to school. With each one he squeezed, he could tell them apart by the way they hugged. Because of the feel of their skin and their different odors, he could see how a blind Isaac could tell the difference between Jacob and Esau in Genesis 27.

As they hug him good-bye, he reflects on each child. *Ruthie's a lot like Mom*, he thinks, *prim and proper, so soft and smooth-skinned*. She wants to learn all she can from Mom; he knows she'll be a fine bride one day. She's one who sees what needs to be done and will set the wheels in motion to accomplish it.

On the other hand, Sara, the eleven year old, is completely opposite; she's the tomboy. If someone can ride a horse, she can. If someone's picking on someone, she runs to their defense. She loves her blue jeans and coveralls and hates dresses. "Dresses are for sissies," she says when Mom isn't around.

Clyde, who's nine and the only boy, has a tough time with the girls except Sara. They hang together all the time, and she pushes Clyde sometimes not in the right direction, but Clyde loves it and says, "She's kinda like having an older brother."

Rachel, the baby of the family, isn't quite sure where she fits in, but she always keeps the family laughing with her antics. Even though she isn't going anywhere, Rachel always lines up for her hug, too.

Sitting there, Dad kisses each child good-bye and reminds them to take a jacket. Just to follow up with Dad's orders, Mom stands at the door and makes sure they button up. It's that time of year when you don't know what the weather is going to do. The old saying in the area is, "If you don't like the weather, wait thirty minutes." Living at this elevation, anything can happen!

Sara grabs her books and quickly says, "Let's hurry down to the road; Mr. Barns might be driving by, and that sure beats walking." Mr. Barns is the delivery man for the hardware and grocery store in town. Sometimes, if his Model T delivery truck isn't too loaded, he'll allow the kids to squeeze in and drive them to the school crossing. You can hear that old vehicle coming for miles.

Elmer says, "Now, you guys; don't be a burden to Mr. Barns."

"Oh no, Dad. He likes giving us rides," Sara quickly responds. Dad smiles and looks at Mom and rolls his eyes.

Chapter 2

Family Feud

As you approach their house, you see the barn on the right with a few stalls for the livestock. The house is further down the road about 50 yards, but it is rather small. The setting is gorgeous with trees all around and a creek running 50 feet behind it. The outside's nothing special to look at, just a typical wooden cottage. Elmer and Walter spent many hours together building it, but one thing they failed to think about was family growth. Elmer spent the bulk of his time working on the inside. The inside walls are knotty pine with a beautiful stone fireplace decorating the front room. The two men gathered the rocks for it from the creek behind the house. The small, front room is furnished with only a few pieces of furniture. To the left of the fireplace is Mom's favorite chair, and straight across from that is Dad's wooden rocker. Across the room from the fireplace is the kitchen table, with the old potbellied stove in the middle of the small kitchen area, with barely enough room for two to walk around it.

The two bedrooms are in the back of the house, one to the left, the other to the right. At the time they built it, it was perfect for their small family, but then Sara came along, Clyde next, and finally Rachel. The result is too many bodies for such a small area. The three older kids share a bedroom, while Elmer and Dorris have Rachel in with them. While small, it's home, and everyone seems to get by.

Once the kids leave for school, Dad turns his attention back to his coffee, biscuits, and gravy. Rachel sits in the corner playing with a couple of toys, and Dorris stands a few feet from the table and turns as if to say something. Elmer senses the same conversation brewing that always seems to take place when he leaves on these property rides and decides to head it off at the pass. He looks up from his breakfast and says, "I have to go," and then thinks, *here it comes*!

"I know, but why not take someone with you?" Dorris quickly counters.

"Honey, we talk about this every time, always just before I leave. Each time my answer is the same. It's best that I go by myself."

"We don't always, and I still don't understand why it's best!" Elmer, with a pained look on his face, swiftly answers, "The ranch needs all the other hands around here to prepare for the coming winter; and besides that, I won't be gone that long. I just need to make sure the fence line is secured for winter!"

Dorris lowers her head, saddened by his response. "I know, but why always you? Someone else could do it once in a while, couldn't they?"

Before Elmer can respond, there's a knock on the door. He stares at Dorris in bewilderment. Who can this be? Walking to the door, he glances back at Dorris and softly says, "I don't want to talk about it anymore!"

Dorris gives him a dirty look and says to herself, "That's fine; I do!"

He yanks the door open, and there stands Walter Livingston with his wife, Maggie.

After greeting each other, Elmer invites them in. While shutting the door, he asks, "Would ya'll like a cup of coffee?"

"Sounds great!" they reply in unison. Elmer turns and looks at Dorris. He can tell by her expression that she isn't too excited about the Livingstons being there. She walks into the small kitchen to fetch a couple of coffee mugs while thinking; *He's leaving for a couple days to take care of your ranch. Can't I have him for just a few last minutes to myself?* She immediately realizes how selfish this sounds and prays to herself while pouring coffee, "Lord, forgive me for my selfishness." Picking up the two cups, she walks to the table.

Elmer, always the gentleman, jumps up and pulls out the chair for his bride to sit down. As Dorris sits, Walter thanks them for the coffee and hospitality. Maggie seems pretty excited about something. She sits on the edge of her chair, leans over, and places both forearms on the table and jumps in, saying, "We have something we want to discuss with you." With this, Walter reaches over and touches her arm gently and gives her a funny look. She returns the look with an endearing smile and sits back in her chair to give him the floor.

Maggie's an excitable lady who always looks for the good in others and situations, which drives Dorris crazy. Maggie believes the husband's the leader of the home and why not? Hers is such a loving and caring man. He truly has a heart for God, and it's a pleasure to serve him. There were times when she thought, *Would I be like this if Walter wasn't the loving man he is?* Her thoughts would roam to other ladies she knew who struggled to submit to a husband who is less than loving, some who were even hostile toward their families. Sitting there staring into space, she quickly returns to the situation at hand and thinks, *Thank you, Lord, for this man You have given me.*

With a smile on his face, Walter turns his attention back to Dorris and Elmer. Dorris prays that Walter will tell Elmer not to go on the ride around or at least take someone with him. Sitting up in her chair, she listens intently to what Walter's about to say.

Walter begins, "Maggie and I are so thankful for the years of dedication your family has given us. We think of your children as our own and want to bless your family." He hesitates for a moment, looks at Maggie, leans over and whispers, "You go ahead and tell them."

Elmer's mind's racing at this point, as is Dorris'! What could this be? Sitting there waiting for Maggie seems to make time stand still—you know, those moments in time which are only seconds, but seem to be minutes long. Maggie gathers her thoughts, rises from her chair, tosses back her long, brown hair while clearing her throat and begins to speak, "Walter and I have been praying, and this place is too small for your family." She continues, her face flushed as though embarrassed, "We want to, as Walter expressed, say thanks for all you have done for us, so we want you to know that we're going to build another home by ours for your family." Elmer looks at Dorris, who returns his glance.

They can't believe their ears. With a look of bewilderment, Elmer questions, "You must be kidding? Why would you do that?"

With the same hesitancy and pride, Dorris responds, "That's way too much for you to do, we can't accept that." Dorris, a very proud woman, works hard for all they have and doesn't look for handouts. Unlike Maggie, Dorris is usually the first to speak when something needs to be said. Most of the time, Elmer allows her to speak her mind, and then expresses his thoughts. But this time, he doesn't wait and jumps right in. He looks at Dorris as if to say, "Slow down," and reaches under the table and touches her leg before speaking.

"Excuse me, Honey, but I must say something here. You two are such a blessing to our family. I thank you for being not just a wonderful boss to work for, but also such a wonderful godly example for Dorris, me, and our family." As he speaks, he watches the different expressions on the faces of the Livingstons.

As Elmer takes a breath to continue, Walter interrupts, "Maggie and I really believe this is what God wants us to do for your family. We've prayed about this and have spoken about it extensively. We're not getting any younger, and we have no family of our own; so please allow us the privilege and blessing."

Watching the Livingstons' reaction, Elmer can tell they're hurt. He reassures them by saying, "Again, we are so grateful for all you've done. We accept your gift and look forward to many more years together." The Livingstons sit back in their chairs and smile from ear-to-ear. Dorris continues to shake her head in disbelief of what she's heard. She can feel her face turning red, but she has to hide her hurt and anger, so she excuses herself from the table while thinking, *How could he do that? Answering without even discussing it with me? What's the matter with him? Who does he think he is?*" She heads to the stove to get more coffee.

Walter stands up, grabs Maggie's hand and says, "We'd better go! Thanks for the coffee, Dorris!"

"You're welcome," Dorris quickly responds. Moving toward the door, Walter looks at Elmer and asks, "You leaving this morning to ride the fence line?"

Elmer answers, "Yep," and tries to get them out the door before the next line comes, but it's too late. "Don't you think you should take someone with you?" Walter inquires.

With that, Dorris makes a beeline to the door where the three are standing and jumps right in, "That's what I told him! I don't really like him going out there this time of the year by himself." "I have to agree with her, Elmer. You need to take someone with you!"

"Alright, you two; don't gang up on me. The other guys are needed here to herd the cattle and get the place ready for winter. The *Farmer's Almanac* predicts a rough winter, and we all need to be prepared. This is just a simple ride around the property. What could go wrong with that?"

Dorris looks to Walter for some kind of comeback, but there is none. Grabbing at Walter's arm, Maggie leads them out the door. Walter cranes his neck and hollers back, "You're the foreman; just know we'll be praying for you."

Elmer follows them out onto the porch, gives a little wave, and shouts, "Thanks!" as the Livingstons head home hand-in-hand. He turns around and walks back into the house. After he closes the door, he can tell something just isn't right. It's not like Dorris to be so quiet. So, being the brave man he is, he asks, "Something wrong? You upset about something?"

That's all she needs, and with raised voice she retorts, "You know what's wrong!"

He responds with his voice not quite as loud, but sterner, "Honey, if I knew what was wrong, I wouldn't have asked."

Feeling the tension, Rachel, still playing on the floor, begins to cry. Mom moves over to pick-up Rachel, and with a cracking voice says, "How could you?"

"How could I do what?"

"Accept their offer without us even sitting down and talking about it?"

"We've discussed this before! Don't you remember? We talked about when and how we'd get a bigger home for the family. I just thought this could be a blessing from God," Elmer answers apologetically.

Dorris, visibly upset and with tears in her eyes, answers, "I know, but I was thinking more along the lines of something of our own, not living on this property for the rest of our lives."

Elmer raises his voice, "Who said anything about being here for the rest of our lives?"

Rachel puts her arms around Mom's neck, gives her a big hug, and buries her face in Mom's shoulder. Dorris shifts into defense mode, "Honey! When you accept a gift like this it always comes with strings attached. You know me, I don't like being beholden to anyone!"

"Now, Dorris," Elmer calls her this when he wants to make a point, "I can appreciate what you're saying, but I have to do what I think is best for the family"

Before he can finish, Dorris jumps in with both feet, "So it doesn't matter what I think, right? The only thing that means anything is what you think is best for the family; is that right?"

"Honey," Elmer responds in a quieter voice, as he attempts to bring this argument to a close.

"Just answer my question, does my opinion matter or not?" Dorris fumes.

After that statement, Elmer fights his emotions. He really wants to let her have it, and thinks, *She's doing the same thing to me she's accusing me of doing to her.* Then a scripture flashes through his mind. He can't quite remember the reference, but it goes "A gentle word turns away wrath." That's what needs to take place. All of these thoughts rush in within seconds; so how is he to respond?

Dorris walks over, sets Rachel on the ground again, and stays at it, "Well, well, are you going to answer me or not?"

Elmer walks toward Dorris, grabs her hand and says, "You know I love you and want to hear your thoughts, but this may not be the time. I have to get going. I will go by Walter and Maggie's and tell them we have to discuss this further, if that's all right with you?"

With a look of disgust on her face, she rolls her eyes and replies, "All that's going to do is make me look like the bad guy. You've placed me in a no-win situation. Thanks."

Elmer isn't getting anywhere, and in order to stay on schedule for his return, he needs to get going. He wonders why things like this always seem to come up just before he leaves for work or for a trip. It never fails!

He stands there next to Dorris, lets go of her hand and takes a moment to try to think of how to best wrap this up. Finally, he says, "I know you're upset. Let's commit this to the Lord over the next few days, and when I come back I will take a few days off and we can lay out our plans for our future. Is that all right with you?"

She answers as she turns and walks away, "Well, I guess so. Not much more I can say or do at this point." While she talks, Elmer walks up behind her and gives her a hug, while kissing her on the back of the neck. He says, "I have 'ta go. I'll miss you and the kids, my bride."

Her only response is, "Be safe." With that, he knows she's still annoyed.

He turns to walk out the door, looks back, and says, "I will always love you. You are the woman of my life."

Dorris acts as if she doesn't hear him, still wallowing in her self-pity.

Too Old, Too Fast

Elmer slips out the door and closes it softly. He walks up to Sacred, throws his right leg over Sacred's back, takes the reins, and guides his faithful horse down the road.

Dorris listens to Elmer's footsteps until they're off the porch. Guilt begins to set in; she begins to think out loud, *How stupid am I? He's not just leaving for a day's work, which shouldn't really make a difference, but he'll be gone for a number of days.* The more she talks to herself, the more panic sets in, and her mind races with "what if" questions. At that point she scurries over, picks up Rachel, and moves to the front door. She reaches for the knob and gives it a mighty jerk because it sticks from time to time, and then finally flings it open. She runs on to the front porch and hastily glances right, then quickly back left, just in time to see Elmer riding away headed north on Sacred. Dorris hollers, but he's out of range. As she squeezes Rachel, she mutters under her breath, "I love you, too. You are the finest man I have ever known."

Chapter 3

The Journey Begins

Elmer rides away from the farmhouse thinking, *What just happened? I can't believe it, we did it again! What's that I hear?* Pulling back on the reins, he brings Sacred to a stop. He tilts his head to obtain the best angle, looks back, and squints his eyes as if it helped him hear better. It must have been his imagination or his desire, though. He sure wished Dorris would come out to stop him. Staring at the ranch, he says to himself, "See you in a couple of days." Sacred turns back around and heads away from the cottage as he prays, "Lord, please be with my family while I'm gone; protect them from harm and help them deal with anything that comes up. Give Dorris peace about what lies ahead. I thank You for the family You've blessed me with and I totally trust in You to provide for us."

At the Y in the road, Elmer decides to go by the Livingstons', since it's close and won't take much time. As he gets closer, he can see the two-story ranch house with a vehicle parked out front. It looks familiar, but he can't quite bring it to mind. Then it finally hits him; it's Patrick Duffy, better known as Pastor Red, pastor of the First Christian Church in town. He's been there since the beginning in 1909, but this past year has been a tough one for the church. The building was destroyed by fire, but the people of the city have banded together to rebuild it.

It doesn't take much to realize where Red got his name with his bright red hair cut closely to his well-shaped head. He has a light complexion with freckles across the bridge of his nose, and he stands around 5 foot 6 inches tall. If you haven't already guessed, he's of Irish descent, and boy, can he preach! Red's presence at Walter and Maggie's is pretty common, since they're one of the main families and supporters of the church. They really love the church, Red, and his family; however, their greatest desire is serving the Lord.

Elmer always seems to find work Sunday mornings; thus, he's not too regular with his attendance, but he makes sure the family goes though. Stopping in front of the house, he dismounts and ties the reins to the hitching post, glancing up to the house where Red and Walter have already risen from the porch chairs and are walking down the steps toward him. They welcome him with a wave, and once close enough; Red greets Elmer with a solid handshake.

"Howdy!" Elmer says.

"Mornin', Elmer!" Red responds.

"Hope I'm not interrupting anything."

Shaking his head, Walter answers, "Not at all; we're just discussing the church rebuild."

"How's that going?"

"Great!" Red interjects, "May be able to have a worship service Sunday. You're going to be there, right?"

"Wouldn't miss it. I should be home by Saturday morning from my ride."

Red looks at Walter, and with a hardy handshake says, "Well, I best be move'n along; need to make sure the building's getting ready."

Walter and Elmer answer back, "See ya later!" as Red heads for his car.

Once Red's gone, Walter looks at Elmer and asks, "What can I do for ya?"

"Well, a couple of things. Would ya mind if Dorris and I think about your offer before we answer?"

"Naturally, Elmer. We want you guys to make sure it's right for your family and something the Lord really wants for you . . . and the second?"

With a look of concern Elmer asks, "If ya could have someone drop by and make sure the family's okay while I'm gone?"

Walter smugly replies, "I've already arranged that. In fact, I think he's on his way now."

"Thanks," Elmer replies, with a sigh of relief, "I'd better be gettin' along, or I'll never make it to the first marker by nightfall. See ya later!"

"Take care and please be safe." Elmer steps over to Sacred and puts his left foot in the stirrup as he thinks, *That's the second time today someone's told me to be safe. That's odd! Oh, well, got to get movin'.*

***

Meanwhile, back at the cabin, Dorris sits at the table crying and talking to herself, "How stupid am I? Why did I make such a big deal about the house before he left? I always seem to do that. I never intend to, but I still do it. If I only. . . . " Before she can finish, someone knocks at the door. Quickly wiping her tears with her apron, she scoots back from the table, stands up, and walks toward the door. She can't imagine who'd be there. If it were Elmer, he'd just walk in. Standing at the door and making herself presentable before opening it, she tugs on the door, but it sticks again. She keeps tugging, and with the third tug, it flies open. Gathering herself together after almost falling over from tugging so hard, she looks up. It's Jonathan, one of the ranch hands. He's new to the ranch and seems to be well-liked. He's a good-looking young man, slender, around 5 feet 8 inches and always polite. Appearances, however, don't always reveal the real person, but he's one who put up a good front. He spends his evenings roaming around town. Others in town already have a nickname for him, *Whiskey*. You see, he lives a double life.

Taking his hat off, he says, "Good day, Mrs. Lewis!"

"Good day! What can I do for you?"

"My name is Jonathan, Ma'am."

"Okay, Jonathan, What can I do for you?"

"Well, ya see, Ma'am, Mr. and Mrs. L sent me over here to look in on ya while your man is gone." As Jonathan continues to talk, Dorris becomes uncomfortable. She watches his eyes and they aren't looking into hers. She's dressed, as always, in a Victorian-style dress, which shows her womanly figure. After all, they never have many visitors, and she always wants to look good for her man. The longer he stands there, the more uncomfortable she becomes, with his eyes wandering up and down and all. By the smirk on his face, she can tell he's enjoying himself, and she wants to get rid of him quickly.

Dorris interjects, "Jonathan, everything's okay; we'll be fine."

"Oh no, Mrs. Lewis, I want to help in any way I can."

Dorris presses the issue, "Jonathan, like I said, we'll be fine. We have plenty of wood and food, but please thank the Livingstons for us. Good-bye." She grabs the door and begins to close it. As she does, he turns to walk away and hollers, "See ya tomorrow!"

She can only stand there and watch this bow-legged young man walk away as she thinks; *He doesn't take a hint too well. I'll have to keep my eye on this one. He's one you can't trust.*

***

It's toward midday by now and Elmer's been riding for a while. He decides to give Sacred a rest and walk a little himself. This part of the fence line is in great condition, as usual, because it's the closest to the ranch house. During the year, as ranch hands pass by and see a break, they'll stop and fix it. It really doesn't take much to fix, as it's made from barbed wire.

The barbed wire used on the ranch has sharp edges, or points, about every four or five inches along the strand. If handled the wrong way, it'll shred clothing or skin; it shows no mercy. There're usually five to seven strands stretching from the ground to around five feet high. The wire's placed between wooden posts, up to half a ton of pressure, so you have to be careful when doing repairs. Depending on the terrain, the distance between posts will vary. On flat ground such as this, the distance may be around 5 to 10 yards. Tomorrow, when Elmer gets to the rougher part of the property, this distance will be cut in half.

The most important part of the inspection is the corner posts. If they give out, it causes slack in the fence, which makes it useless. Replacing a corner post is tough for one man, but it can be done. Elmer has the expertise to handle anything that comes up.

When doing this type of work, you need plenty of gloves, since handling this stuff will destroy a pair rather rapidly. There are too many tools and repair supplies to carry on horseback, and a wagon can't go to some of the places they need to, so they've built small storage sheds around the property. While serving for storage, they can also serve as shelter in time of need. They're not very big; in fact, only big enough for two guys to lie down in. Even then, they have to turn over together or they'll be hitting each other. This is one reason Elmer likes coming by himself. He can't get much sleep when someone's along, and with all the manual labor, sleep is a necessity.

Riding now toward dusk, Elmer enjoys watching the sun's descent into the western sky. He thinks back to home and the many nights he and Dorris would sit outside watching the sunset, and he says a short prayer for the family. With the sun rapidly setting, he figures he can't make it to the next shed, so he looks for a place to set up camp. It doesn't take long to find the perfect place.

After pitching his small tent, he sits outside and gazes into the western sky. What a beautiful sight! There's a small pond about ten yards away where he sees a mirror image of the sky reflecting a clump of evergreens in the distance. Just above them, the clouds are bright yellow with red swirls mixed in. Above the clouds, shades of blue paint the sky, progressing from light blue to the darkest overhead, stretching across the entire horizon.

"What a perfect painting to end the day. Lord, please be with my family while I'm away," Elmer prays as he settles in for the evening and prepares for tomorrow.

Mom and the kids scurry to finish chores before they lose daylight. As Ruthie leaves the barn and heads to the house, she notices the sunset.

She sprints toward the house, 'cause these types of pictures don't last long, and hollers, "Mom, come outside and look at the sunset! Hurry!"

All Mom hears is Ruthie screaming, so she runs out with a scared look on her face. "What is it Ruthie? What's wrong?"

"Look at the sky!"

"Ruthie, you nearly scared me to death over a sky?"

"Just look, Mom."

"Oh, my, that is beautiful! Look at all the colors, the yellows, reds, and blues."

"I hope Dad's watching," Ruthie says.

"I'm sure he is. I'm sure he is," Mom replies with a knowing smile. Her Elmer loves the sunsets, and she's sure he's not missing this one.

Elmer gets his fire going for the evening. He finds some small rocks to make a small circle with, just enough to contain a fire. There's an abundance of twigs around to keep it going for quite some time. He reflects on his family and knows that by now they're all home and sitting around the table sharing an evening meal. With a smile on his face, he opens his saddle bags and pulls out dinner for the evening. It hasn't even been one night and he's already missing Dorris' home-cooking. In the saddle bags, he finds a treat and a note from Dorris that reads:

"To my love, I hate not having you around for these next few days. I will miss you more than I can describe. So you don't miss us much, I've packed you a surprise. Please eat them the first night as they may not be good longer than that. I love you, my man!"

He takes a gander into his saddle bag and sees something wrapped in a towel. A smile crosses his face as he unwraps a small towel containing three homemade biscuits, his favorite. He sure loves his woman! The stars peek through the black skies overhead as he leans back against an old log and eats his biscuits. As he looks at the sky he remembers something from long ago; can't remember where he heard it from, but it goes something like this, "Starlight, star bright, first star I see tonight." He stops there with a laugh 'cause he can't quite put the rest of it together.

***

Mom finishes preparing the evening meal as the kids complete their chores. As they sit down at the table, Clyde takes over, "Since I'm now the man of the house, I'll pray." He commences, "Lord, please help us to eat this food and protect us, and be with Dad as he's away and bring him home safe, Amen. Now let's eat." Ruthie passes the food around, while Mom asks how the day went.

Whiskey heads to town, but stops about half way and thinks *I'm going to check on the Lewis's.* Making a wide turn, he heads back to the small house. Not wanting to draw attention, he parks by the barn. He slowly walks toward the house and steps on the front porch. Hearing voices coming from inside, he stands there and listens intently to what they're saying. Being a little confused about what to do next, he notices the kitchen window and decides to walk over and peek in. On his tip-toes, trying not to make any noise, he moves to the window and squats as to not be seen. Little by little he inches upward until his eyes are just above the window sill. He sees the back of Mrs. Lewis sitting at the table with the kids. Moving around the table with his eyes, he notices the oldest daughter. She's one cute, shapely dame, just like her mother, and he can't take his eyes off of her. He ducks under the window and thinks *I'd better get away from here before someone sees me.* Slowly, he backs off the porch and approaches the front door.

Inside the conversation hits its peak, but Mom senses someone at the window and cocks her head to listen but doesn't look. As she listens she whispers, "Hush for a moment!" With the conversation at full volume, few hear her plea. Finally, she states emphatically, "Please, be quiet! I think I hear something." With that, the kids immediately hush and look at each other with concern. As all ears strain to hear the slightest noise; you can hear a pin drop.

The silence is interrupted by a loud knock at the door, which startles the girls into letting out a horrific scream. It's so piercing that Clyde covers his ears with his hands and hollers, "What's wrong with you? It's just someone at the door!" Before anyone realizes it, Mom's at the door. Her instincts were right, someone was watching, but who can it be? She slowly opens the door and peeks through the crack. She can't believe who's there.

***

The fire dims as do Elmer's eyes. He slips into the tent, crawls into his bedroll, and thinks; *Tomorrow's going to be a busy day. This part of the property has always had the most damage. I must be about a half mile from the next shed, since each is about two miles apart. I have to be on the alert, 'cause this part of the property has the easiest access for rustlers. We're out in the middle of nowhere. It's easy for them 'cause they can see people coming for miles. Need to get a good night's rest so I'm also prepared to not get bushwhacked.*

***

She opens the door wider, "Good evening, Jonathan, what can I do for you?" Her anger boils within.

"Good evening, Ma'am; thought I'd check in and make sure all is fine."

"We're fine, just like I said earlier. We don't need any help, and if we do, we'll let the Livingstons know."

As the conversation continues, Mom can tell he's not looking at her, but looking past her as he speaks. She observes his eyes tracking Ruthie, the oldest daughter. Now her anger is really boilin'. She tries to control her emotions, but thinks, *First it's me, and now my daughter; I need to run this guy off and warn Maggie.*

"Please don't put yourself out, we're fine."

"Oh, no problem at all, Mrs. Lewis," he responds as he cranes his neck in an attempt to look around Mom and get an eyeful of Ruthie. Mom keeps moving, however, in an attempt to block his view.

"Thanks again for coming by, Jonathan, but I have to go now. Have a lovely evening." Mom closes the door and leaves him standing on the porch.

Ruthie says, "Mom, that was rude. I don't think I've ever seen you act that way."

"I know, but he won't take no for an answer. You all be careful when he's around. I don't trust him."

"Oh Mom, don't be so suspicious!" Ruthie exclaims.

"Just do what I ask, period," Mom retorts.

Ruthie sits back in her chair and folds her arms, visibly upset over how Mom just spoke to her.

Jonathan steps from the porch, walks back to his car by the barn and drives away. As he heads to town, he begins to talk to himself, "I don't think Mrs. Lewis cares for me. What have I done to her? I'm only trying to help while Elmer's away. Boy, that older girl sure is a doll; I'd love to get to know her. Mom can't protect her forever. I'll just bide my time."

The closer he gets to town, the more he can taste that first drink. It's always the best one. He stops behind the Western Drake Hotel and tries to keep a low profile as he slips into the bar through the back door. Built in the 1880's by an insurance company to accommodate potential settlers, the hotel is magnificent. With a fireplace in every room, and a large dining hall, it's one of the most elegant places for miles around. Located downtown at First and Broadway, it's definitely out of place for this small community.

Jonathan approaches the bar and the bartender greets him, "Evenin' Whiskey, your usual?"

"Yeah, thanks!" The bartender hands him his bottle and he heads up to his room. As he walks up the stairs, he thinks *Another long day tomorrow, but maybe I'll see that Lewis girl. I wonder what her name is.*

Chapter 4

Danger All Around!

As the sun tops the horizon on this beautiful Friday morning, Mom hauls wood into the house. The weather got a little brisk overnight, so she needs to get things warmed up. Her thoughts go to Elmer and she shoots off a little prayer, "Lord, I pray he's warm and hurries home." The kids slowly make their way out of bed, not their normal energetic selves. Clyde's the first to the table and is very lethargic. Sara sits down next, and places her head on the table. Ruthie scoots up to the table and stares out into space. Rachel's the only one who acts like herself this morning and who talks a "mile a minute" while the others just sit there like lumps on a log, waiting for breakfast.

Mom stands at the stove in her usual position, watches the kids file in and asks, "Okay, you three, what's wrong?"

Ruthie's speaks up first, "We didn't get much sleep last night!"

With a puzzled look, Mom asks, "Why, what happened?"

Sara contributes, "Well, with Dad gone and all, and with what happened last night when Jonathan came by, I guess we're all just a little scared."

"Yeah!" Clyde pipes in, "We've never seen ya act like that to anyone. It's not like ya, Mom!"

Sara adds, "When we went to bed, we talked, and it looks like you don't like him. Mom, tell us what's wrong!"

With a reassuring smile, Dorris explains, "I'm so sorry you didn't get much sleep last night! I wish you had said something. It's not that I don't like him; it's just that with Dad being gone and all, I'm a little on edge. I can see that all of us are." She surely isn't going to tell the whole story of how Jonathan makes her feel. If she does, they probably wouldn't sleep well until Dad got home. "Please forgive me for scaring you guys. Dad'll be home tomorrow, Lord willing, and I can't wait."

"I miss him too, Mom!" Ruthie responds.

Clyde interjects, "I know; I can't wait 'cause we get to go on an overnighter together. Oops, never mind."

"Clyde, what's that about an overnighter?" Mom inquires.

"Oh, nothing; it's just something between us men," Clyde responds.

The girls look at each other, roll their eyes and giggle. The thought of Clyde calling himself a man always makes them laugh.

"You'll see. You won't be doing that when Dad gets home!" Clyde snaps back.

"Now, now, Clyde. The girls didn't mean anything by it. Did you, girls?"

The girls promptly look at each other and know what they have to do, or else be in trouble with Mom. "No, Mom, we're just teasin'."

"See, Clyde; they're just teasing you. You all better get a move on now, or you'll be late."

"Yeah, let's hurry! Maybe we can catch another ride!" Sara pipes in.

***

It's still dark when Elmer climbs out of the bedroll. As he gathers his things, he prays for the family, and then makes his plans for the day. *Don't have much time to spend gathering wood for a fire, which means a hot breakfast is out. What really sounds good is a nice warm cup of coffee. Oh well, I just need to get going so I get a full day's work in*, he thinks to himself. The briskness bothers him some. It's not supposed to be this brisk this time of year. "I pray this isn't an indication of what's to come." He saddles Sacred and, as the sun rises, heads up the fence line.

The next section of fence is a mess. Between rustlers and falling tree branches, a lot of the line posts are down. While still a lot of work, it's a blessing that none of the corner posts need replacing, so Elmer gets busy replacing the line posts. This is the most common fix, and material is easy to find; he can use thick tree limbs, miscellaneous pieces of wood, or just about anything. There are three trees that are native to the area—Boxelder, Cottonwood, and Hackberry. The one most commonly used for line post is the Boxelder that average twenty-five to forty-five feet tall, while the Cottonwood averages forty to sixty feet in height; and lastly, the Hackberry, related to the Elm, grows to a height of forty to sixty feet. Elmer doesn't have to look far to find material for repairs.

After a few hours, this section is secure and it's time to move on. Not far up the trail, he comes to one of the small sheds and makes a short stop to stock up on gloves, having already worn through his first pair, along with other materials. As he starts to close the door, a noise catches his attention. Standing still for a second, he hears the sound of horses' hooves pounding the ground. He instantly remembers what part of the ranch he's in and knows it probably isn't anyone he knows or wants to. Before leading Sacred into a gully not far from the shed, he quickly grabs his rifle. The shed's only ten yards from the fence line, so Elmer has a clear view of who's coming.

***

Jonathan wakes in a daze. He's overslept again and is going to be late for work for the third morning in a row. These late nights are getting to him.

"I'll think of another excuse on the way, but for now I need to get going," he says as he grabs his clothes and runs out the door.

C. E. Andrews

Driving to the ranch, the perfect excuse dawns on him: "I'll stop by the Lewis's place. That'll be a great excuse." As he approaches the road that leads to the cottage, he sees the kids walking to school.

He pulls over and asks, "You guys need a ride to school?"

Ruthie says, "Oh, no thanks; we can walk."

Jonathan pleads, "Ah, come on! The Livingstons sent me by to make sure you all get there safe."

"Great! If the Livingstons sent you, then we'll take a ride!" Sara exclaims.

"Thank the Livingstons for us," Clyde replies.

"Sure will, now hop on in so we can get going. There's not much room, so you'll have to squeeze in," Jonathan smirks. Sara and Clyde stand there waiting for Ruthie to get in. At first she doesn't want to, but she slides over while the other two squeeze in next to her. The back seat's full of saddles and other tack equipment, so no one's getting back there. Ruthie's far closer than she feels comfortable, but the other two are thrilled to not have to walk.

Jonathan feels Ruthie's warmth next to him and notices her sweet fragrance. He thinks, *Wow, I never thought I'd be this close to this beautiful young lady, not so fast, anyway*! Not wanting this to end, he drives as slowly as possible, but unfortunately, the school is in sight. As they pull up, the other two kids quickly pile out and Ruthie slides toward the door. The others run off without even saying thanks, but she turns and looks into Jonathan's bloodshot eyes and says, "Thank you for your kindness." As she reaches her hand out to shake his, it doesn't take him long to grab it. They shake hands and he thinks, *What soft lovely hands; so expressive when she speaks.* She closes the door and Jonathan watches her walk away. He can't get over how beautiful she is and how well she carries herself. Ruthie walks up the schoolhouse steps, turns, looks back, and gives a little wave. Well, that's all the encouragement he needs to allow his mind to run away. The rest of the morning he runs that moment over and over in his mind.

Walter walks out of the bunkhouse as Jonathan pulls in to the driveway. Jonathan can tell he isn't happy. As he gets out of the car, Walter walks up.

"You're late again, Jonathan. I can't have this."

"I'm so sorry, Mr. Livingston." Jonathan replies.

"Jonathan, you either get your act together, or you're gone. Understand? What's the excuse this time?" Walter admonishes.

"I understand, Mr. L, but you told me to look in on the Lewis family and that's where I've been. They asked me to drop them off at school, so I had to go back into town. It won't happen again."

Walter's chin drops to his chest as he responds, "Oh Jonathan, I'm so sorry! You're right; I did ask you to do that. Thank you so much for taking care of them! I feel so bad."

"Don't feel bad, Mr. L. We all make mistakes. I'm just trying to be a servant."

***

Elmer ducks down in the gully, peeks back over the edge and sees three riders approach the fence line. He leans against the side of the gully and notices that he left the shed door ajar. What will they do if they notice it? One rides up to the barbed wire, dismounts, and scouts along the fence line, while the others lag behind. They all act as though they've been here before. As he gets closer, Elmer thinks, *I know these three! I've seen them in town before.* He observes one of the men on horseback point to the open shed door and then begin to look around. He says something ever so softly to the other rider. Elmer strains to hear, but he can't figure out what's being said. Just then the third rider shouts, "Hey, the shed door's open. Someone must be around here. Let's ride!" The scout runs back, jumps on his horse, and they high tail it out of there. Elmer thinks, *Thank you, Lord. I don't know what I would have done if they'd stayed. This just puts me further behind, though.* He walks over and locks the shed, retrieves Sacred, grabs the saddle horn, pulls himself up, and then heads north.

C. E. Andrews

Elmer moves along at a good pace. While there's a lot of fence to mend, it doesn't take as long as he thought. Along about midday, he can tell the weather's turning by the rippling sound of the leaves in the trees and the threatening gray cloud cover forming over the highest mountain peaks. As he rides, he pulls his Stetson down further on his head to keep the wind from blowing it off. He passes several sheds and thinks; *Maybe I should stop here for the day. Those clouds don't look too good, and it's getting pretty chilly.* Giving it further thought, he concludes, *Nah, I can make one more shed . . . not many repairs along here anyway. Shouldn't take much longer, besides, I'll be that much closer to home.* He reaches back into his saddlebag, grabs his duster, and puts it on. After a couple of stops to mend the fence, the weather really turns south and he decides, *This is the last fix of the day; I'm headed to the next shed.* Observing his whereabouts, he figures he must be right in between sheds, so it makes no difference whether he goes forward or back. He decides to press on. It shouldn't take long to get there, but by the time he finishes the repair, the wind's gusting so hard, it stirs up dust devils, making it hard to keep his hat on. He quickly mounts Sacred and thinks; *I pray I haven't waited too long ta head to the next shed!*

By this time the wind and rain are blowing in his face, and it's getting harder to see by the minute. Thinking he can get farther along on foot, he dismounts and leads Sacred along the fence line, but soon he realizes it's useless to try and go any farther, so he scans the immediate area for shelter. With visibility down to almost nothing, and the temperature still dropping, snow must not be too far behind. He can't believe this is happening, and thinks, *This trip's been wrong from the beginning. I should have listened to the others. What else can go wrong?* Only time would tell.

***

Back home, Mom goes outside to fetch more wood and notices the sky. She thinks, *When I was out here a couple minutes ago, the sun was shining and the sky was blue. This doesn't look good; it's changing in a hurry*. Then her thoughts focus on the kids. *They're walking home from school. What should I do?* She begins to panic. *Dad's gone and the kids have to walk home. What are they going to do with this weather changing so fast? This could be a risky situation for them.* Watching the weather change before her eyes, she says under her breath, "It's looking pretty nasty." Then she reflects, *I wonder where Elmer is? Is he safe?* She rationalizes, *Oh, he's been through this before; he'll be fine, but I'll pray anyway.* "Please, Lord, guide and direct him and show mercy on him in this weather. Amen."

Her thoughts are driving her nuts! She feels like a yo-yo, going back and forth between the kids and Elmer. *I have to stop doing this; first things first*, she thinks as she walks back into the cottage. *The kids need my attention right now. If Elmer were here he'd take the car and pick them up, but I don't drive. What should I do, Lord?* Then it hits her, *I'll call Walter.* She walks over to the kitchen wall and picks up the phone, but before she can rouse anyone, she hears a car coming down the gravel road. Hurriedly, she hangs up, steps out on the porch, and sees the store's delivery truck headed her way. She strains to see who is in the cab and lets out a sigh of relief as she sees all three kids in the front seat with Mr. Barnes. The winds really pick up, blowing so hard the barn doors are slamming, and the gate to the corral is opening and closing by itself. Off in the distance she can see the rain starting to fall. She thinks, *It won't be long before it's here and with the temp dropping, we're headed for some snow.* Dorris stands on the porch, her hair blowing to one side and her skirt blowing so hard the hem's almost at her waist. Mr. Barnes pulls to a stop and the kids hop out and run into the cottage. Dorris walks up to the driver's side window, looks at Mr. Barnes, smiles, and says, "You're an answer to my prayers!"

"Well, I know the mister is gone, and since ya don't drive, the kids needed to get home somehow."

Dorris gratefully responds, "Thank you so much! I don't know how I'll ever repay you. I owe you, and I will pay you for your trouble."

"Don't worry, it's no big deal," Mr. Barnes replies, "Gotta run an' get back before this storm hits. Looks like it could be a nasty one! See ya'll later."

Mom says good-bye and turns to look for the kids. They're already in the house trying to get warm, but Mom knows there's a lot of work to get done before the storm hits. The animals need to be secured, along with the house and barn.

Mom opens the front door and yells, "Let's get a move on. We need to get this place buttoned up!"

"Mommmmm," Clyde responds.

"Don't, 'Mom' me!! We have a lot to do! Get a move on!"

Mom barks out orders, "Clyde! You and Sara make sure all the animals are in the barn and the barn doors are closed. Ruthie, you help me close the storm shutters on the windows. We also have to get a bunch of firewood in the house. We're not sure how long this is going to last."

"Yes, Mama," they all respond.

Clyde and Sara rush out the front door while Ruthie runs outside to close the shutters on the house as Mom locks them from inside. Clyde runs through to the back of the barn and pulls the doors toward him. Almost on cue, a gust of wind blows through and swings the doors wide open, flinging Clyde right out the back of the barn. He hollers for Sara and she comes running and grabs one door as Clyde gets up and grabs the other. They pull them together and Sara holds them while Clyde lays a plank across the two to hold them shut.

The front doors will be the easiest, they think. They're walking to the front, when Clyde realizes the loft door is still open. As he scrambles up the ladder, Sara hollers, "Be careful, Clyde, that's a long way down."

The wind howls as Clyde climbs the ladder, muffling Sara's voice to where he can't understand her. Clyde gets to the loft door and notices rain is starting to fall. The door is wide open and laying against the face of the barn. In order to secure it, Clyde must reach out and grab the rope that's swinging in the wind. He spits on his hands, rubs them together, and reaches for it. Just before he grabs it, the wind blows it away. He repeats this a couple more times with the same results. Finally, throwing his hat off to the side and rubbing his hands together, he takes one more lunge and grabs the rope. There's only one problem, he's off balance. With his arms outstretched and his feet barely hanging on the last board of the loft, he tries to pull himself back in, but to no avail. Stretched out there, with the wind blowing and trying to stay balanced, he knows he's about to tumble out the window. Sara walks up behind him, grabs him by the waistband of his Levi's, and gives a mighty yank. Clyde tumbles back, the door closes, and Sara secures it with a piece of wood. Clyde looks up at Sara in relief and says, "Whoa! That was close! Thanks, ya saved my hide."

"That's what I'm here for, little man," Sara says with a smile.

They head back down the ladder and Clyde runs out the front door, pushes it closed, and makes sure the latch is firmly in place. The wind's been slamming the side door against the barn pretty good, so Sara props herself against it. Clyde hops on the coral fence and herds the animals through the side door. It doesn't take much for most of the animals to come running. They know a storm's brewing, but there's a few that Clyde has to run down. Once they're all in, Sara secures the side door, and they hurry out the corral gate, locking it as they leave.

Mom and Ruthie are having a tough time with the shutters. Ruthie's holding them closed and getting pretty wet in the process while Mom's having a tough time locking them because the locks are old and hard to latch. They're finally down to the last one, the one by the kitchen. In frustration, Mom reaches over, picks up a frying pan, and gives it a couple of short taps. That does the trick! By now the rain's coming down in sheets, and with the temp dropping, it doesn't take long to turn to snow.

In the meantime, the other two are bringing in firewood from the other side of the cottage and they're soaked to their skin. Each time they go around the corner, the wind blows the rain in their faces. They put their chins to their chest and press forward with all their strength to get the next armload. It's not only the wind they're fighting, but the rain is now blowing almost horizontally. It hits them like needles poking them all over. They're tired, wet, and hungry.

After making numerous trips, Clyde asks, "Sara, is this enough? I'm tired."

Sara hollers, "The more the better. I don't want to come back out to get more."

Clyde replies, "I think we have enough. The one wall in the house is piled up as high as I can reach."

"Okay, just one more armload," Sara promises.

So off they go for one more trip. Mom looks at all the kids have done and hollers, "Sara, that's plenty! You guys get on in here."

Sara, Ruthie, and Clyde all walk in the house together, soaking wet. The girls' hair hangs down like wet noodles, and Clyde stands shivering. As Mom looks at them, a smile spreads across her face as she says, "You guys look like a family of drowned rats! Get out of those wet clothes, and I'll build up the fire for you to warm by."

***

Elmer knows he's in real trouble and is not too sure what to do. The first place of refuge he thinks of is the gully, but with flash floods always a threat, they'd be swept away in no time. Sacred starts getting real uneasy, which is not like him. He tries to comfort him, but that doesn't work. With no place to go, Elmer starts to dig a small foxhole close to the fence and under a tree for shelter. He thinks, *I'm above the water level, and if I cover myself up, I should be okay until this one blows over. Sacred will have to deal with the elements on his own.* As he digs, the wind dies down somewhat, but the clouds still look ominous. Sacred is right there next to him as the rain hits, pouring, as they say, "raining cats and dogs." The wind picks up again as Elmer digs frantically, and then he hears a loud crack and turns just in time to see a main branch of the tree snap off and head right at him. He hollers, "Oh, my Lord!"

Chapter 5

Bad Moon
On The Rise

As the storm worsens, Mom and the kids sit by the warm fire. They hear the wind howl as they sit around and talk. In the middle of their conversation, Clyde leaps to his feet and blurts out, "What about Dad? He's out in this!" Mom was wondering how long it would take for one of the kids to bring up Dad.

"Your dad's been in storms like this before. I'm sure he's safe in one of the supply sheds, waiting out the storm. He'll probably get home a day or two late."

"You sure, Mom?" Ruthie chimes in.

"Yeah, remember Dad's lived in this weather most of his life," Mom replies.

"I sure hope so!" Ruthie says.

"Me, too," Sara and Clyde join in.

Mom thinks to herself, *Me, too! Elmer's a brilliant man who always seems to know what to do and is hardly ever wrong.*

After thinking for a moment, Mom says, "Why don't we pray for him right now?"

Without hesitation, Clyde says, "Since I'm the man of the house, I'll lead."

As Clyde bows his head, Ruthie smiles at Sara. It always amuses them when he says things like that, but this time it just seems to fit.

Clyde springs right into prayer, "Lord, please help my dad. Keep him safe and warm, and please get him back to us soon as possible. Amen."

Once Clyde finishes, Ruthie follows, "God, you know how much Papa means to our family. Please protect him through this storm and get him home safe to us."

Sara cuts in with, "Jesus, thank You for our home and the wood to burn to keep us warm. I pray for warmth for Papa and a shelter to protect him. Amen."

Mom concludes, "We thank you, God, for listening to our prayers, and we look forward to having Dad home soon. Amen."

The family regularly attends church and listens to Reverend Red preach. Boy, can he preach! While he stirs up their emotions, a lot of times what he says doesn't make much sense, but they all believe in God. They're not as religious as some folks and the Livingstons are definitely more religious than they are. They know they're good people and God would never turn His back on good people.

After finishing their prayer, through the howling wind they hear someone come up on the porch, and then knock on the door. Mom looks at the kids and, with her hands motioning up and down to let them know to stay put, she gets up and walks to the door. She thinks, *Who would be out in this weather? Whoever it is they need shelter quickly!*

***

Elmer watches as the large main branch heads toward him. Time seems to slow down to a crawl. It's as if someone has put everything in slow motion. He tries to move, but it feels like trying to move in quicksand. He hollers, "Oh, God, the branch is going to hit me!" He turns and throws his right arm up over his head in an attempt to protect himself. At the last possible moment, Sacred steps in between Elmer and the huge branch, and takes a direct hit to the side of his head. Elmer looks back from under his arm just in time to see the mighty blow and cringes at the sound of it. Even with the howling wind, he hears the horrible thud, which sounds like someone striking a water barrel; Sacred immediately falls to his front knees as Elmer hollers, "Nooooooo." Sacred wobbles for a few seconds, then attempts to stand back up, first with one leg then the other, while whining and snorting blood. Unable to stand, he finally gives in to the sharp blow and falls to his side.

While Sacred slowed the branch's momentum, it didn't stop it. Cracked and swinging in the wind, Elmer notices it is only attached to the tree by a small piece of wood and bark. The swinging action along with the weight of the branch won't keep it attached to the trunk for long. Elmer takes a step back to avoid the limb, and thinks, *Alright, I dodged that disaster.* As he steps back, though, he steps into the hole he was digging and loses his balance. He falls back and hears another large crack. It's the branch as it breaks away. Falling flat on his back, and hitting his head on the ground, he now lies there watching the branch head directly at him. He quickly wiggles his way backward, trying to get out of the hole and out of the way of the branch. He's fast enough to get his upper body out of the way, but not fast enough to get his right leg out of the way, and the branch falls across it. Even through the howling wind he hears a mild snap, and then immediately pain shoots up and down his leg.

He's been bucked off horses, bulls, and almost anything you can ride and been trampled by Brahmas, but he's never experienced this amount of pain before. He lies there screaming as loud as he can, with the huge branch across his leg. The wind seems to turn into a whisper. The world spins out of control; he knows he's close to blacking out. His eyes roll back into his head. As he slips into unconsciousness he thinks, *I can't take this pain anymore!*

***

Mr. Livingston calls the ranch hands together to inform them of the impending storm and to instruct them about what needs to be done to prepare for it. With Elmer gone, Walter directs the men, "Make sure the horses and other animals are securely placed in the barn and the storm shutters are on the windows of the home and barracks. If the storm shutters don't get up, we'll be replacing windows for the next few days." As they head out, he assigns each a task and tells them to assist others who need help when they finish. The ranch hands complete the jobs and head to the barracks for shelter.

Walter and Maggie are sitting in the parlor talking when the front of the storm hits.

Maggie looks at Walter and asks, "You sure Dorris and the kids are okay?"

"No, I'm not; didn't have time to send anyone."

With a look of disgust, she sarcastically replies, "What cha mean you didn't have time? You had enough time to get this place ready!"

Walter's emotions rise and he thinks, *I've worked getting our place ready; I can't take care of everyone.* His face reddens, but he stops and prays, "I was only thinking about protecting our place. I took nothing else into consideration. Lord, please forgive me for this." Then he tells Maggie, "I know, but to tell you the truth, I've been so busy around here, I never really thought of sending someone over there. Please forgive me?"

That's what Maggie loves about her man. He can admit it when he's wrong. She sympathetically answers, "That's okay. You know, I didn't think about it till right now, either; but we should pray for them and Elmer. I hope he's found shelter."

***

After completing his jobs at the ranch, Jonathan heads back to town. Walter tries talking him out of going, but he really wants to get back to his place. As he travels the two-mile journey into town, he thinks about Ruthie and what happened earlier in the day. He thinks, *They may need my help. Even if they don't, I can see her again.* He decides to head on over to the cottage. Probably not the smartest thing he's ever done, but, oh well!

Too Old, Too Fast

***

The wind's blowing so hard that Dorris has a hard time opening the door. As she holds it tightly with both hands, she sees a man's silhouette on the porch. There stands Jonathan, soaking wet, and anger wells up within her.

She angrily asks, "What can I do for you, Jonathan?"

"Well, Ma'am, after I finished up at the Livingston's, I thought I might come by and help ya'll secure the place from the storm. Sorry, it took a little longer than I thought to get here. Then my car got stuck in the mud, and I had to walk the rest of the way."

Dorris' anger vanishes immediately, replaced with compassion for him. After all, he was trying to do something nice. "Thank you so much, Jonathan! You can see we're safe and secure, but if you stay out there much longer you won't be. You'd better come inside." The kids look at one another and can't believe their ears. This is the same lady who only last night treated him so rudely.

Jonathan thinks, *It worked! I get to see that beautiful young lady again!* "Thank you, Ma'am!" he gushes as he steps inside.

***

The rain quickly turns to snow as Elmer regains consciousness. His right leg throbs as he lies in the hole, pinned down by the log. As he comes to, he hears himself moaning in pain. His initial thought is, *I must be dreaming*, but it doesn't take long for reality to set in as the next shot of pain shoots through his leg. He lets out another scream as his mind races a mile a minute. In an attempt to put things together, he blinks, slowly shakes his head, and recalls the sequence of events. *I heard that first crack of the branch, and then fell back into the hole, slammed my head on the ground and with th e last snap the branch fell across my leg. It's all real, not a dream. I must have passed out. I wonder how long I've been lying here.*

His sight's blurred as he looks around; his thinking is unclear, but he is rational enough to realize he's in some serious trouble. Dorris' warning pops into his mind, "Don't go by yourself." He thinks, *I should have listened to her, doggone it! Oh well, that's water under the bridge. Gotta figure out what ta do next.* The only thing he can do is pray for wisdom. "Lord, Ya there? I really don't like this situation; in fact, this really ticks me off and scares me. What should I do? How am I going to get this thing off my leg? I don't understand."

A mixture of snow and rain is coming down pretty steady. Then it hits him. Where's Sacred? Elmer sits up the best he can and tries to focus. He scans his surroundings, looking left then right, and squints again to focus. Finally, he spots Sacred lying a few feet away. He tries to move, but the tree limb has him pinned. Each time he tries, the pain's excruciating. Sacred's breathing is labored, and there's blood all around from the vicious blow to the side of his head. About that time, his pain reminds him of the dire situation he's in.

***

This storm's one of those that comes along once in a decade, especially this time of the year. While Jonathan warms up next to the fireplace, he can tell the family's uncomfortable with him being there.

Mom finally breaks the silence, "Well, Jonathan, where are you from?"

Jonathan's taken aback by the question. He can't remember the last time someone asked him a question like that. Stuttering his way to an answer, he thinks, *Do I tell the truth or should I make up a story?* He answers, "Well, Ma'am, I was born in southern Oklahoma, but I lived mostly in Texas."

Wow, that felt good to tell the truth! I should try it more often, he chuckles to himself.

"Are your parents still alive?"

"Not quite sure, Ma'am."

The answer seems to bother Dorris as she gives a little wrinkle of her nose, which Jonathan quickly picks up on. He immediately thinks, *See what happens when you tell the truth? That's why it's always best to not let people get too close by telling it.* As the conversation continues, it seems that Mrs. Lewis is checking him out, with questions directed toward his personal life. Jonathan repeatedly tries to change the conversation to no avail. Finally, sensing Jonathan's frustration, Ruthie intervenes, "Mom, let's get dinner ready. It's getting late."

"I know, I know."

Clyde jumps in with, "Yeah, Mom, I'm starved!"

Jonathan thinks, *Thank you, pretty lady. Ya saved me*! He's having a hard time keeping his eyes off her.

Clyde comes up to him and says, "Thanks for the ride to school today!" Mom isn't sure she heard things right, so she just ignores it and goes on preparing the evening meal. Ruthie turns her head and glares at Clyde, then takes a swift glance at Mom to see her response. She doesn't notice any changes in Mom and thinks, *Great, Mom didn't hear him.* At the same time, Mom's controlling any emotional response, thinking, *This isn't the time to make a big deal over this, we'll deal with it later.*

***

Elmer can tell this is going to be one nasty storm. As the temperature continues to drop, the strong wind blows the snow into big drifts. Elmer's tried everything he can to get the log off his leg. He tried using his left leg to roll the branch, but it's so heavy he can barely budge it. The snow starts piling up, and with the wind; the wind chill factor is 5 to 10 degrees less than the temp. Elmer knows that in order to survive, he needs to free himself. Sacred begins to stir, and Elmer thinks, *If Sacred can help, we can get back to the shelter before the brunt of the storm hits.* Elmer examines Sacred from a distance and concludes that he doesn't look too good. Though his body seems to be in pretty good shape, the branch hit him squarely on the right side, and from his viewpoint, it looks as though it did some pretty major damage. The right eye is bashed in, and Elmer's not sure if he can see or not. There's quite a bit of blood, but in order to survive, Elmer has to get Sacred up.

He starts encouraging Sacred, "Come on, boy, you can do it." Sacred stumbles to his feet, wobbling as he stands he walks over to Elmer and leans his head toward the ground. Elmer prays he doesn't fall over and crush him, and then thinks, *If I can get him to get this branch off my leg, we might just stay alive.* As Sacred stands there, Elmer notices how mangled that right eye is. There's no way he can see out of it. With Sacred's nose within arm's length, Elmer strokes his brave horse's nose as blood drips off the end of it. Elmer gently moves Sacred's nose toward the large branch and encourages him to move it. Sacred gets the idea almost immediately and begins to roll the branch. Elmer's pain is almost unbearable. As the branch rolls off his leg, he lets out a scream, which scares Sacred to a stop.

Gaining his composure, Elmer encourages Sacred to continue. With each roll, pain shoots throughout his body. He starts to think about what's going to happen when this huge log gets to his foot. If he doesn't do something, as it rolls it will likely break his ankle. He places his hands under his leg and positions his body to move it so he can roll to his side. This will allow his foot to lie flat on the ground. The log begins to roll by itself now, and Elmer needs to make his move. As the log gets to his ankle, he gives a quick turn, and his foot rolls to the right. With that there's another huge shot of pain, and again he feels light-headed, as if he's going to pass out. He fights the pain, knowing that if he passes out, it may be all over. The log rolls off and he's still conscious. Sacred takes a few steps to the right and once again falls over. Elmer looks down at his leg. He can tell it's broken, and the skin's peeled back from the log rolling off. At least he's free. Now all he has to do is get up on Sacred's back and get to the next shelter. Things are really looking up.

Chapter 6

The Horse

Dinner is done and cleaned up and, since it's Friday; it's family night. A number of years ago, Dorris and Elmer started gathering the family on Friday evenings to play checkers, chess, or the girls' favorite card game, Old Maid. Once the game time ends, there's a family sing-a-long time as Sara plays the harmonica. The kids always argue about which games they're going to play, Clyde the loudest.

Clyde challenges, "Who wants to get beat at checkers?"

"Oh, you think so," Sara responds in her normal quiet voice.

"You bet cha; I'm the champ!"

Mom, still in the kitchen cleaning up, shakes her head and thinks, *Clyde's already at it. Oh well, it's a normal Friday night—well, almost normal.* She's uneasy about Jonathan being there when Elmer's gone, but what can she do? He's their guest.

Ruthie walks over to Mom and asks, "Anything I can do for you, Mom?"

In a quiet, but stern voice, Mom questions, "Yes, tell me about this ride to school!"

Ruthie's taken aback by the question and acts very defensive. That immediately tells Mom that Ruthie knows what they did was wrong.

"Well?" Mom repeats herself.

Ruthie stammers for the right words to say. Jonathan, sitting on the floor across the small room, reads Mom's lips and concludes their conversation is about the ride this morning. Curiosity gets the best of him. Trying to hear what's being said, he casually scoots closer to Clyde and Sara. They're getting pretty loud as they play checkers on the floor, so he can move without being too obvious. The old copper pie safe is in the perfect position to hide behind. The pie safe's about 4 feet tall, so sitting behind it or even lying on the floor watching a checker game is perfect cover. He listens intently to what Ruthie's saying.

"Well, we were on our way to school and Sara's looking for Mr. Barnes. Mama, you know how much she hates to walk all the way to school. Then all of a sudden, Jonathan pulls up out of nowhere and asks if we want a ride. At first I refused, but Clyde and Sara say, "Sure!" and jump in. I didn't want to, Mama, but I did it for the sake of the other kids!"

"Well, we'll take care of this tomorrow morning!" Mom says sternly.

Oh, my! Jonathan thinks, How do I get out of this one? I'll have to play it by ear and look for a way out.

Dorris really doesn't want to handle this. She's hoping Elmer will be home early tomorrow so he can deal with it. She walks over to the window and stares off into space, thinking about her man, *Where are you, are you safe? How close to being home are you? I have so many questions, with no answers.*

While she stands there gazing out the window, Clyde walks up and puts his arms around her waist and says, "Mama, you okay?"

"I'm fine, my little man."

"What cha thinking about?"

"Just the storm and how bad it's going to get."

Clyde senses the worry in Mom's voice and tries to encourage her, "Mama, Dad's going to be okay. Ain't no storm he can't handle. Besides, we already prayed, and God's gonna take care of 'im."

Too Old, Too Fast

Dorris looks down into those beautiful blue eyes, and all she can do is smile. This young man has enough faith for both of them. With tears in her eyes, Mom responds, "I know, my little man, I know."

Clyde loves it when she calls him her little man, although he thinks, *I ain't so little. After all, I'm nine now, almost grown up*. He still likes hearing her say those endearing words, though. Overall, Mom's not very affectionate; none of the kids can recall the last time she told them she loved them, but they always know it to be so.

"Who won the checker game, Clyde?" Mom asks.

"Sara did, but she cheated."

"How'd I cheat?" Sara asks.

"You jumped more than one man at a time, and that's not fair."

Sara knows it's useless to try to tell him that's part of the game, so she just lets it go.

With a smile, Mom tells the kids, "Time to clean up for family sing-a-long."

***

The snow's falling and blowing at a rapid pace. Even though Elmer's thankful for his brave horse, right now he needs him to stand. He thinks, *Once Sacred stands, I can lie across the saddle and he can take me to the supply shed.* Elmer grabs hold of the bridle and gives a tug. Sacred lets out a loud painful whinny, raises his head, and wobbles to his feet, bringing Elmer to his feet as well. Never had he heard such a screeching noise come from him. Elmer thinks, *Now to try and get up on his back.* He grabs the saddle horn with his left hand and steadies himself with his right hand against Sacred, lifting his left leg to the stirrup. He pulls with his left arm and pushes down with his left leg to raise himself up. Unable to swing his right leg over, he flops across the saddle on his belly. Lying there he thinks, *This is going to be a tough ride for the next half mile or so, but at least I don't have to walk or crawl.* His thoughts turn to home. *It's late Friday afternoon and the family's probably preparing dinner. Within the next hour dinner will be cleaned up and they'll begin to play games. Clyde likes checkers and I always let him win. Then he struts around bragging about being champ and says, "Who wants to get beat?"*

Just thinking about it brings a chuckle. Ruthie's probably helping Mom with dinner and Sara's taking care of Rachel. *What a great family. Thank you, Lord, for such a caring family*, Elmer concludes. Sacred slowly begins the journey to the shelter with the wind howling through the trees. The snow falls like a dense white blanket, difficult to see through. *Once I get to the shelter, what will I do with Sacred? I can't think about that, we may not even make it.*

Sacred's none too steady as Elmer encourages him to keep going, "Come on, boy, you can do it." They don't get far, about 100 yards down the path, when Sacred begins to shudder and Elmer knows what will follow. He has to do something fast so he won't get trapped under Sacred when he falls. With his forearms he pushes off Sacred's back just as he collapses to the right. He slides off the saddle, the easy part, but landing's not. His good leg takes the brunt of the fall and it's all he can do to keep the other one up. Unfortunately, no matter how hard he tries; his broken leg still hits the ground and sends pain shooting throughout his body. Too much pain to stand, his good leg buckles and he crumples to the ground next to the barbed wire fence. Lying there holding his leg, he's thankful he didn't fall into it. Elmer looks at Sacred, who's only a few feet away, and can tell he's laboring to breathe. He scoots over to his faithful horse that has given him all he can and says to himself, *This horse has saved me numerous times. We've labored side by side for years. He's truly my best friend, and here he lays suffering.*

Elmer chokes up as he evaluates Sacred. Blood is coming from his mouth and nose. The noises seem to be uncontrollable; from the grunts to the shrill screams, he can tell he's suffering. It's just a matter of time, and Elmer knows what needs to be done. He lies next to Sacred, and with his right arm, reaches over to the saddle holster where his Winchester is. Leaning against Sacred to reach the butt of the rifle, Elmer feels him struggle to breathe. As he thinks about what he must do, tears flow down his cheeks. Every now and then Sacred neighs in great pain. With rifle in hand, he pulls himself up to his feet with the help of Sacred's body. Sacred repeatedly tries to raise his head, but to no avail. Elmer stands over Sacred, sees his beloved horse's only good eye looking up at him and weeps bitterly. He can hardly hold onto the rifle as he shakes uncontrollably. Sacred begins convulsing and Elmer says, "Enough is enough." He lifts the rifle, takes aim and, with his right index finger shaking, pulls the trigger.

Sacred is gone. It's as though the shot has quieted the wind and the weather is being held back. Elmer hears the echo of the shot go on for what seems forever as he stands over Sacred. Nothing else seems to matter as he drops the rifle and falls to the ground. He wraps his arms around Sacred's neck and cries, "I'm so sorry. Thank you for being such a faithful friend. There will never be another horse like you. I'll see ya over yonder."

The snow's drifting up all around them, but Elmer stays until he feels the warmth begin to leave Sacred's body. Finally, he sits up, looks around and thinks, *I'm in real trouble. I have no transportation; the weather's getting worse, I can't walk, and with close to a mile to go . . . whoa there. Slow down; let's take this one step at a time.* Elmer takes a deep breath and thinks, *Okay, first things first. Now that I have to walk, I need to set and splint my leg.* Knowing he'll need something to tie the splints to his leg with, he takes out his pocket knife, cuts the saddle bags, bridle, and reins from Sacred and looks around for pieces of wood. Barely able to see, he crawls toward the fence line where there just happens to be two pieces of wood in plain sight that'll do the job. Elmer thinks, *Okay, what next? I've got to set my leg.* He prays he can take the pain and set it right, or he'll cause more damage. It must be done!

His hands and legs are numb from the cold. He can't recall ever being this cold, with no relief in sight. Every once in a while, he blows on his hands, rubs them together, and then on his pants in an attempt to keep them warm. At times, it feels like someone's poking them with tiny needles. He thinks, *How will I set my leg? I have to get something to tie it to that won't move. Maybe the fence? No, the force may break the post.* As he looks around, it hits him; *I can use Sacred's legs.* Still unable to crawl, he scoots back to Sacred's front legs. Placing his broken leg between them, he tightly ties his leg to the horse's, knowing the dead weight will prevent Sacred from sliding as he falls back. This may be enough to set the bone. He thinks, *It's worth a try.* Elmer secures his leg to Sacred's and then prays, "Lord, in order for me to survive, I need Your help. Please allow my leg to set correctly."

As he concludes, he rises to a squat with his bad leg out. Then, with one quick jerk, he kicks out his left leg and falls to his back. First, there's a loud pop, then bone-smashing pain, followed by an agonizing holler. He reaches down, clutches his leg with both hands, and unties it from Sacred. Once free, he lies back and rolls in the snow as tiny little stars appear to flash all over. He blinks repeatedly in an attempt to make them go away. Now lightheaded, with his head throbbing and his stomach churning, he thinks, *I'm going to throw up any second now.* He knows he can't lose consciousness or he'll freeze to death.

The snow's coming down harder and drifts continue to pile up. Taking deep breaths and slowly exhaling, he gradually gains his composure and realizes his leg actually feels better. It's a relief, but scary at the same time. He thinks, *It either set right or it's numb from the cold. Either way I have to splint it.* He wraps it in the saddle blanket and then places the two branches on each side of his leg. Using Sacred's reins, he cuts the leather straps into four cords, long enough to wrap around his leg and secure the splints. Unable to feel his fingers, he ties them the best he can. He thinks they're secure enough to stand. Supporting himself, he stands, saying to himself, "It feels okay, but the real question is, can I walk?"

It becomes perfectly clear after taking that first step that as he puts weight on his leg, over he goes. The snow and rain make it impossible for him to walk, even with a homemade crutch. Lying there once again in the snow, he thinks, *Okay, that's not going to work, but I have to do something to get to the shed before sundown. If I don't, I'll never find it in the black of the evening. So many things are going against me, I have to persevere. I must keep going for the family.* With this in mind, he reflects back to his family. *They're probably done with dinner and games by now and are gathering to have the family sing-a-long.* With a smile he thinks, *Boy, Sara does a great job leading the sing-a-longs. It's good for building her self-confidence, too.* Sara, being the second born, is always the odd one out. With Ruthie being the oldest, Clyde the only boy, and Rachel the baby, they always seem to take the spotlight. This is Sara's time to shine.

***

As everyone gathers in the open room, they all seem a little preoccupied. It's anyone's guess what they have on their minds, but Mom's sure that some are missing Dad. The kids move around slowly, acting like they don't want to sing tonight. Mom encourages them to hurry, thinking this may make everything seem normal. As Mom passes by the kitchen window, she hears the howling wind. Stopping and peeking out through the storm shutters, she sees the snow falling and thinks, *It's still daylight, but when the sun goes down, the storm will only get worse. Elmer, I pray you're safe.* Not wanting to draw attention by standing at the window too long, she begins to move and suddenly feels the presence of someone walking up behind her. There's a gentle touch on her shoulder that sends shivers down her back. As she turns, she sees Jonathan, and it makes her skin crawl.

"Ma'am, you okay?"

"I'm fine, Jonathan! Please go over there with the children."

"Just want to make sure all is fine."

"I said it was; please go!"

As Jonathan walks away, Mom turns back to the window and says under her breath, "Please hurry home, Elmer. I need you."

C. E. Andrews

***

The sky's still bright toward the end of the day as snow continues to pile up and Elmer tries to find a way to get to a shed. Whatever he does, he knows he has to do it soon, so he begins to slowly scoot on his rear. The snow blows directly into his face as he heads toward the shed. He thinks, *I should be about a half mile or so from the shed, and with any luck, I'll be there long before dark* The more he tries, the slower he goes, fighting his own body weight while sinking into the snow. With every scoot forward, all he does is make a bigger pile of snow to scoot over. After a few minutes, he realizes this isn't going to work. It will take far too long. He's still not able to use his right leg without causing extreme pain. He has to think of something else, something that will act as a sled to go over the snow.

As his energy wanes from the strain of attempting to scoot, a thought comes to him. *If I can lie on my back and use it like a sled, I could move along on the top of the snow, but how can I only push with one leg?*

The snow continues to mound, and Elmer gets colder and wetter before he comes up with an idea. *If I lie on my back, pull myself with my hands and use my good leg when I can, that should work. Now, what can I grab to give me leverage?* He looks around and sees only one thing he can use—the barbed-wire fence.

Scooting toward the fence, he recalls, *The barbs are 4 to 5 inches apart, and if I'm careful, I can grab in-between the barbs and not hurt my hands. It's a shot I have to take.* He has a pair of gloves on and another in the pocket of his trench coat. *These should be enough to get me to the shed,* he thinks.

Reaching the fence, which is only feet away, he makes his first grab and pulls. *It seems to work okay,* he thinks. He takes another grab, then another, and another, and pulls himself along for a couple of minutes, thinking, *This is going to work great! Thank you, Lord.* Moving along now at a good pace, he reflects back to home. *By this time, they're starting to sing.*

Too Old, Too Fast

One of his favorite songs is "Red River Valley." He sings as he scoots along:

"From this valley they say you are going.
We will miss your bright eyes and sweet smile.
For they say you are taking the sunshine
That has brightened our path for a while."

He sings as loudly as he can to drown out the wind and cold, along with the pain.

***

Finally, Mom has the family together. Sara grabs the harmonica, sits on the floor in front of everyone and asks, "What song do we want to sing?"

As they look around at each other, Clyde jumps in, " 'Red River Valley,' that's Dad's favorite."

Sara sees tears well up in Mom's eyes, so she hurries to start the song. She plays like she's never played before; she wants the others to sing to take their minds off the weather and Dad. As she belts out the song and the family sings along, the second verse really stands out,

Come and sit by my side if you love me.
Do not hasten to bid me adieu,
But remember the Red River Valley,
And the cowboy who loved you so true.

Mom begins to cry, not out loud, but enough that she turns away from Rachel, who's sitting on her lap.

***

Elmer's moving along at a good rate now, and then it happens; what he's been afraid of. He gets caught on a barb. Instead of in-between, he accidentally grabs a barb. It penetrates his glove, and as he jerks away, it takes some skin with it. His hand begins to bleed, and he lies there for a second in pain, and then returns to singing and moving forward.

> *Won't you think of the valley you're leaving.*
> *Oh how lonely, how sad it will be?*
> *Oh think of the fond heart you're breaking*
> *And the grief you are causing to me.*

Pulling along, he looks back and notices pieces of his glove still hanging on the barb. With each pull from his right hand, he can now feel the steel wire. His strength is quickly fading, which means now more than ever, he catches his hands on the barbs. With the gloves torn apart and his fingers being so cold, he feels less and less pain. The only warmth he can feel is from the blood oozing from all the cuts on his hands and fingers. He can't believe he's gone through two pairs of gloves in such a short period of time. His good fingers form blisters from all the pulling, and he doesn't know how much longer he can go. He thinks, *The shed must be getting close.*

***

Sara notices Mom has turned her back, and she loses a note or two herself; but composes herself enough to finish the song.

She quickly asks, "What do we sing next?"

Chapter 7

Survival Mode

Ruthie can't recall a time when the family hasn't gathered together on Friday evening. They're always great times with games, singing, and Mom reading from the family Bible. Tonight's different, though, with Jonathan here and Dad gone. Ruthie wonders if Mom's going to read tonight. Sitting on the floor in front of Sara, looking down, Ruthie gets an awkward feeling. It's something she can't explain or recall ever having before. Raising her head, she gives a quick glance in Jonathan's direction, and sure enough, he's looking right at her. He smiles and gives her a nod. This isn't a normal nod and smile. Ruthie thinks, *That sure seems like an unusual smile, not one I've seen before. Wonder what's going on in his mind?* What she doesn't realize is that he's flirting with her, but she doesn't have a clue. All she knows is that she's very uncomfortable.

***

Elmer continues his journey, pulling himself along the barbed-wire fence. By now he's almost totally exhausted and has to stop every four or five tugs to rest. The only thing that keeps him going is his thoughts about his family. While pausing to rest, another song comes to mind, "A Cowboy's Best Friend Is His Pony." He blurts out the first verse, hardly able to get through it with his emotions running so wild. His adrenalin kicks in, and he starts pulling harder as he sings:

> *A cowboy's best friend is his pony,*
> *Yes sir I can prove it to you.*
> *One day I was lost in a blizzard,*
> *My pinto was faithful and true.*
> *—Wilf Carter*

***

Sara repeated, "Next song?"

Clyde again speaks up, "A Cowboy's Best Friend Is His Pony."

Mom nods her head in agreement; it reminds her that her man isn't alone out there. Mom thinks, *Sacred will do whatever possible to keep Elmer safe. What a great horse!*

She reflects back to when they first got him. Skinny as a rail and under-nourished, he belonged to some drunk, drifting cowboy who had gotten himself into financial straits and needed some money to pay off his debt or else. Elmer saw in Sacred not just a horse but something special. He used the extra money they had from Dorris's sewing for town folk to purchase him. It didn't take long to have this horse in tip-top shape. Elmer's great with animals and Sacred's quite aware of Elmer's love for him. By the time Mom gets back from reminiscing to the song, they're already singing the second verse. She sings as loudly as she can with a newfound sense of hope,

> *We were out riding after some dogies,*
> *Many a mile we had gone,*
> *And we knew by sun-up that mornin'*
> *That we were sure in for a storm.*

***

Elmer's moving along at a good clip now, even though his hands are cut and bleeding. With the last verse of the song, he begins to weep again:

Too Old, Too Fast

When we ride on the ranges in Heaven,
It's the roundup on that judgment day,
Up there we must prove true and faithful,
When sent out to gather the strays.

Just thinking of Sacred is painful. He's been pulling now for quite some time and isn't sure if he's going to survive this bitter cold. Everything about him seems frozen: his boots are soaked from the snow, and his clothes can't absorb another drop. Totally overwhelmed with pain, hunger and cold, he stops and cries out, "Lord, I can't take any more, I've had it! Do with me as you will. I'm tired, weak, cold, and hungry. What more do You want? I need somewhere to lay my head and get a little warmth, but I can't find the shed." He looks to his left and thinks he sees something. It's mostly buried by a snowdrift and not far from the fence, but could it be a shed?

***

Rachel sits on Mom's lap and, as always, is pretty fidgety for some reason, though this last song calms her. She acts as though she's singing along. As they finish the last verse and sit around talking, Rachel slides down from Mom's lap and walks over to the chair by the window. She crawls up, peeks through the storm shutters, and with a mournful voice cries out, "Poppa, Poppa!"

***

Elmer crawls over to the mound and begins digging with his hands. "Yes, it's a shed, hallelujah!" he hollers. His energy seems to return, and even though his hands are frozen, he digs furiously and finally gets enough snow out of the way so he can open the door. His emotions run high as he thinks, *I'm only a few moments away from being out of the elements*! He reaches for the handle, pulls hard, and the door begins to swing open when something charges out of the shed and leaps right at him. Elmer throws his arms up to protect his face and a raccoon hits the top of his Stetson, causing it to fly off. He tries to grab it, but it lands just out of reach. Elmer thinks, *I'm getting out of this weather! I can always get another hat.*

He quickly empties the shed of all the fencing material, and with a little daylight left, inspects the inside of what will be his home for who knows how long. Looking around, he spots a blanket in the corner, some old clothes, and another pair of boots, which he prays will fit. He thinks, *This stuff must have been left by the last guy who stayed here.* Crawling inside, he closes the door just enough to get out of the wind and still have some light. He can't wait to get out of the wet clothes, so in between shivers he peels them off. Still not able to bend his leg, he unties the splint and cuts his pants off. This takes twice as long to change. The dry clothes are quite a bit larger, which makes them easier to put on and much more comfortable. As he attempts to redo his splint, he decides not to put the wet saddle blanket back around his leg. It may dry and add warmth if the temperature dips any lower. Once organized and comfortable, at least as comfortable as he can be in this small place, he closes the door the rest of the way and prays, "Thank you, Lord, for your continued provision and this dry place." Then he recites the Twenty-Third Psalm: "The Lord is my shepherd; I shall not want. He maketh me to lie down in green pastures: he leadeth me beside the still waters. He restoreth my soul: he leadeth me in the paths of righteousness for his name's sake. Yea, though I walk through the valley of the shadow of death, I will fear no evil: for thou art with me; thy rod and thy staff they comfort me. Thou preparest a table before me in the presence of mine enemies: thou anointest my head with oil; my cup runneth over. Surely goodness and mercy shall follow me all the days of my life: and I will dwell in the house of the Lord for ever. (KJV)"

It's great being out of the weather. Lying there, he listens to the howling wind and some feeling starts to return to his body as his shivers slowly dissipate. While out of the wind, it's still not that warm in the shed. Leaning back against one of the walls, the hymn "Amazing Grace" comes to mind and he sings:

Too Old, Too Fast

Amazing Grace, how sweet the sound,
That saved a wretch like me!
I once was lost, but now am found,
Was blind, but now, I see.

***

The kids begin to cry and Mom, trying to keep her composure, walks over to Rachel, picks her up, and gives her a big squeeze. She walks back to her chair with Rachel in her arms. In an attempt to make things light, she says, "Let's sing another song. How about Amazing Grace?"

"Sounds great!" Clyde quickly chimes in, "That's my favorite," and leads off as loudly as he can. Ruthie looks around for Jonathan, who's sitting on the other side of the room. He doesn't know the words and is pretty self-conscious just listening to them. The family begins the second verse and you can tell they're getting pretty tired:

'Twas grace that taught my heart to fear,
And grace, my fears relieved;
How precious did that grace appear
The hour I first believed!

Mom wonders where Jonathan is with God. Does he believe, or does he know anything at all? His face seems confused about *grace* as he listens. She thinks, *I need to talk with him about Christ.*

***

As Dad sings, the words seem to stand out more than ever before. He thinks, *What a perfect song for my situation.*

Through many dangers, toils, and snares,
I have already come;
'Tis Grace hath bro't us safe thus far,
And grace will lead me home.

C. E. Andrews

The Lord has promised good to me,
His Word my hope secures.
He my shield and portion be
As long as life endures.

This has been a day of days, one he never wants to repeat, like two or three wrapped into one. He lies there thinking, *If not for the storm, I'd be home early tomorrow. I know I'm not far from the house, maybe seven or eight miles, but instead I'm stuck here until the storm passes.* With no mode of transportation he really has no way of getting home. He can't walk, and has few rations left to survive on. About the only thing he can pray for is that this storm passes quickly and they send out a search team for him. As he begins the last verse, with his energy totally drained, his eyes become heavy and he nods off to sleep while singing:

When we've been here ten thousand years,
Bright shining as the sun,
We've no less days to sing God's praise
Than when we first begun.

***

This song took the life right out of the family, and Clyde looks pretty tired as well. Ruthie tries to avoid Jonathan's glances, and Sara's pretty dry-mouthed from playing the harmonica. Mom looks around the room and knows it's going to be hard to keep everyone awake for the Scripture readings, but she needs to try.

She proclaims, "Let's spend a couple of minutes reading the Bible!"

The children roll to their bellies, and with their heads in their hands, look intently up to Mom as she opens the Scriptures. Jonathan, not wanting to get involved, stays on the opposite side of the room. He thinks, *Is this really what families do?* He can't recall any of the places he grew up in doing anything like this. It's a little strange, but not too bad . . . tolerable. From the time he was eleven or twelve, he got shifted from one place to another. His early years were about the same; Mom and Dad didn't seem to stay in one place too long. One day they moved to a new place, and the family stopped at a restaurant for dinner. When they sat down to eat, his dad got up to go to the head. A few minutes later Mom got up, kissed him on the forehead, and said she was going to wash her hands. That's the last he saw of either parent.

He's still ashamed and embarrassed. As he ran that back through his mind, it makes him angry all over again. He thinks, *I'm so bad that my own parents don't even want me. I must be one evil guy. No one will ever get close enough to hurt me again. I can't trust anyone. In fact, the only thing people are good for is to get what I want from 'em.* He really gets himself worked up, and continues thinking, *Now I have to sit here and listen to someone read me some silly little fairy tales out of a book that comes from who-knows-where? I'm sure Ruthie can't believe this stuff; all this "God stuff" is too much for me.*

As Mom reads the Scriptures, the children begin dosing off one by one; first Rachel, then Clyde, and finally Sara. Mom ends her Bible reading with John 3:16: "For God so loved the world, that he gave his only begotten Son, that whosoever believeth in him should not perish, but have everlasting life." (KJV)

That's the first verse Ruthie ever learned, and she always loves hearing it. Mom puts the Bible down and asks her to help put the kids to bed. Naturally, she obliges. She loves helping Mom do most anything. Rachel hardly moves as Ruthie picks her up and adjusts her head on her shoulder as they disappear into Mom and Dad's room (Rachel sleeps with Mom when Dad's gone). Mom reaches down and shakes Sara by the shoulder in an attempt to waken her. Her eyes open, but it looks as though no one is home. Standing her up, Mom turns her toward the back of the house, picks up Clyde, and heads that way herself. Jonathan finally moves out from the far corner. On her way back, Ruthie grabs a couple of blankets for him. She begins the conversation with, "Here are a couple of blankets for tonight. Thanks for looking in on us."

"No problem, it's different from what I'm used to."

"What do you mean?"

"Well, all this 'God stuff'; ya don't really fall for that, do ya?"

"What . . . you don't believe?"

"Are you kidding me? I'm way too mature for all that God stuff. That's only for weak people."

With this, Ruthie becomes irritated. "We're not weak people! In fact, my dad is one of the strongest men I know. You wish you were as strong as he is!"

"Whoa there, little lady; didn't mean to ruffle your petticoat or anything. I just meant that it's not for me. Don't need it, can handle my life quite well, thank you."

As Mom enters the room to say good-night, she knows Ruthie and Jonathan have been engaged in conversation. She can feel the tension, but not quite sure why. It'll have to wait until morning. Mom says, "Time for bed. Say good-night."

As Ruthie and Mom head off to bed, Jonathan plans how he'll get out of the next morning's conversation with Dorris. He thinks, *Can't be here when morning comes, or I may be found out. I'm tired; just need some sleep.*

Chapter 8

The Wait

It's Saturday. As the sun tries to peek through the clouds, and snow continues to fall ever so lightly, Mom dresses to prepare breakfast. The kids are sleeping in as she slowly opens the door leading into the main room. Walking gently as to not awaken Jonathan, she spans the room. All she sees is a pile of blankets folded in the corner. Jonathan's nowhere to be found.

***

Jonathan awakes just as the sun begins to rise. Peeking out the front window, he sees that the snow has lightened and decides it's time to leave. He thinks, *I need to get outta here before anyone gets up.* As quietly as he can, he folds the blankets and stacks them in the corner. He tries to open the front door, but despite his gentle tugs, it sticks. Finally, he lifts the handle and the door gives way. He walks softly out of the house, slowly closing the door behind him. Walking toward the barn to get his car, he notices snow piled up to the top of the tires and thinks, *That's not going anywhere for a while. Maybe I'll borrow a horse from the barn?* Stopping for a second to think it through, he decides, *On second thought, they may consider that horse-stealing, and that's a hanging offense*. It doesn't take long for him to decide to walk to the Livingstons'.

***

Elmer's not sleeping well. The temperature continues to drop, and the blanket left in the shed has seen better days and is not providing much comfort. Sacred's blanket isn't dry yet, and it really isn't large enough to keep him warm anyway. He wraps up the best he can with what he has. Throughout the night he tosses and turns trying to keep warm. While in a half-conscious state, his mind races about being rescued. *How long will it be before they come looking? Will they send just one guy? Where will they look? When will the storm stop?* There are so many questions and really no answers to be found; it's all in the hands of the Lord.

The shed's one of the older ones in disrepair. Rebuilding the sheds will be a priority next spring. He shivers from a breeze finding its way into the shed. He can't quite figure out where it's coming from, but he continues looking around and thinks, *It's probably just my imagination!* Then he recalls, *Wait a minute, a raccoon leaped out at me when I opened the door. That means he had to get in here someway. There must be some sort of hole or loose board.* Trying to focus his eyes the best he can; he takes another look around but with no luck. He lifts his hands about his head and begins feeling for maybe a hole or loose board. With his hands in pretty bad shape from the barbed wire, it hurts just to move them, especially when touching the side with his fingers. Finally, with his right hand he feels something. Sure enough, there's a hole up by his head. He'll have to fix this, or who knows what else will try to get in out of the weather?

***

Jonathan (Whiskey) reaches the Livingstons' ranch house just as the sun breaks through the clouds. He's chilly from the walk, so he heads straight for the bunkhouse to warm up. This freak storm has made a mess of the place and will put them behind schedule getting ready for winter. As he walks in, the other hands give him a hard time.

"What happened to you? Did you lose your way *and* your car?"

"Yeah, Whiskey, too far gone last night to remember where ya parked your car?"

They're all having a great time laughing at him when Mr. Livingston (Walter) walks in and everyone becomes quiet. They all know that if Walter ever finds out about Whiskey's other life; he won't be working much longer. Walter doesn't put up with that kind of behavior from his hired hands. He's pretty straight-laced and expects the same from his men.

Mr. L, as the hands like to call him, looks around and announces, "Let's get ready; we have a ton of work to do. There are repairs from the storm that need to be made, along with the regular preparation for winter." Mr. L looks straight at Jonathan and says, "Jonathan, I need to speak at ya, if I could, please. The rest of ya get to business." The ranch hands head out of the bunkhouse as Walter turns to Jonathan, "Jonathan, I was in town yesterday and heard some rumors! If they're true, we really need to talk about them!"

"Like what, Mr. L?"

"Like you've picked up a nickname, Whiskey, because of all the drinking you do. Is this true?"

His mind begins to race, *What do I say? If I tell the truth, he'll probably fire me; if I lie, he'll find out sooner or later, and then I'll get fired. What to do?*

After stammering for a second, he says, "You know rumors, Mr. L. Someone starts them and then it gets blown way out of proportion."

"Well, I hope so, Jonathan. My wife and I like ya and want what's best fer ya. It's something that concerned us, and I needed to talk to ya about it. One more question for ya. Have ya ever heard about God's Son, Jesus Christ?"

Oh, here it comes, thinks Jonathan. *I heard this last night and now again this morning. I'm about to hear how much God loves me and all that other religious stuff.* "Oh, sure I have," he replies.

"Have you ever made a decision?"

"Decision? Decision about what?" he asks.

Walter gets a concerned look on his face and Whiskey, thinking fast, says, "Oh, oh, I know what ya mean. Well Sir, my mom always went to church and I'd go with her, so yeah, I made the decision!" Naturally he's lying. He never went to church with his mom. If all the facts be known, his mom never went to church either. Jonathan just doesn't want to be preached at. He thinks, *Why can't people just keep their religion to themselves? Why force it on people like me?*

"Well, Sir, if you don't mind; I need to get to work. The day is burning."

"Sure, Jonathan, but just know if you ever need to talk, just come a callin'."

"Yeah, thanks, Sir; I will." As he turns to go, he thinks, *What would I ever need to talk to you about besides work? You don't understand what I've been through and all you would do is judge me, like the rest of those religious people.*

***

Dorris begins making breakfast for the family while looking forward to Elmer's return. One by one the kids come out of the bedroom, eat breakfast, and start their chores. You can tell they're just as excited about Dad's return as Dorris. They're taking special care in doing their chores, making sure they're done just perfect for Papa. As the morning turns to afternoon, the family fears that Dad might not make it home today. Mom doesn't want to bring it up, so she goes about her activities without saying much. As late afternoon drags on, Mom repeatedly glances out the kitchen window to see if Elmer might be riding in. Standing at the window, she can see if someone's coming off the open range for quite a distance. She's turning to walk toward her bedroom when a knock comes at the door. She races to open it, and there stands Walter with a big smile.

He greets her, saying, "Afternoon Dorris, is Elmer home?"

"No, I haven't seen him yet. We thought he'd be home by late morning or early afternoon."

"Well, no need to worry; the storm probably put him behind. If ya would let me know when he comes in, I'd appreciate it."

"Sure will, Walter; thanks."

"Oh Dorris, by the way, the church ain't quite done yet, so we'll be meeting at our usual place in the morning."

"Thanks, Walter. We'll be there."

"Have a great evening," Walter says as he walks away.

"See you tomorrow," Dorris replies as she closes the door.

***

Elmer's been in the shed about twenty-four hours now, and he wants to get out and stretch. He turns his upper body toward the door and gives it a shove. It doesn't open! *What's wrong with this thing?* he wonders. As he continues to push, it dawns on him, *I had to dig to get to the door, and since it snowed overnight, the snow must be blocking it. All I can do now is just lie here and wait.* His throat's a little scratchy and his nose is draining. *I must be comin' down with a cold.* All he has to chew on is beef jerky, but he does have a full canteen of water, which he's being very cautious with. "Oh Lord, please send someone to look for me soon," he prays.

***

As the kids settle down for the evening, no one dares to ask about Dad. Ruthie can tell Mom is worried. Her answers are short, and she paces around the house. Ruthie is cautious not to add to her concerns and takes the others aside to explain the best she can why they shouldn't talk about Dad not being home. She rationalizes, "After all, the snow's the cause of Dad being late, and he'll probably be here before we leave for church in the morning."

***

Lying there in the shed, Dad thinks he hears movement outside. He listens carefully to what sounds like some kind of animal moving around the shed. With the hole and the loose boards around it, any animal can try to get in, so he lies as still as possible in order to hear any other sounds. All of a sudden it sounds like someone or something scraping along two sides of the shed. *What could it be?* Elmer ponders, *I've never heard anything like this before.* Listening ever so intently, it finally hits him. *Something's digging down to the shed through the snow. Maybe someone has found me? Or maybe not, it may be something I don't want in here.* Just in case, he decides to move away from the hole. The noise gets louder and louder, when all of a sudden a snout pokes through the hole and begins to move the siding. Elmer can tell from the snout it's a wolf. It smells his scent, and with a deep bass-like growl, indicates it wants in.

A minute later another is at the door, biting at the shed's siding, trying to tear it off. Dad reaches for his rifle. Again the first wolf sticks its nose through the loose board. Elmer takes the butt of the rifle and pounds it into its nose. The wolf immediately leaps back with a squeal of pain. The other one at the door isn't having much success, but it's going to be a long evening if he can't rid himself of these animals.

As he tries to figure out what to do, the wolf at the hole becomes quite irritated and makes a final bid to get in. Elmer steadies himself as the wolf musters all his strength and tries to get through the hole. He gets his head in far enough to grab Elmer's pant leg and begins to pull. He takes the rifle and aims at the gray wolf but hesitates, not wanting to shoot himself. The animal's teeth scrape his leg, causing four long gashes, so he rapidly responds with a shot. The wolf lets out a loud cry in definite pain and steps back from the shed opening. Elmer hears some commotion outside as other animals draw near their fallen companion. He thinks, *What are they doing? I know that sound; it's familiar.* As he listens, he determines that they're eating and with his heart racing he thinks, *I must have killed the damn thing and the others are feasting on him. Well, at least they'll leave me alone.* He now needs to fix the shed as best he can. So to work he goes, using the materials that are left in the shed. Fatigued from the day's events and labor, he suddenly gets the chills, this time the teeth-chattering chills. They only last a few seconds and he drifts off to sleep praying, "Lord, please don't let that wolf have rabies."

**

Dorris can hardly wait to get home from church. She expects to see Elmer there at the house and looks around for Sacred as she walks up to the house. When she doesn't see him, she knows something is wrong. She tells the children "Go to the house; I'm going over to the Livingstons'." She saddles up one of their horses and heads over. As she heads up to the Livingstons' front yard, she notices Walter and Maggie walking toward her with unusually somber faces.

He greets her, "Dorris, is there something I can do for ya?"

"Yes, Walter, we need to go find Elmer. I feel there's something wrong. He's now two days overdue!" With that, she can't hold it together any longer and breaks into tears. Maggie walks over to Dorris and puts her arms around her.

In a sorrowful voice Walter says, "Dorris, it's too late today, but I'll get the hired hands together early in the morning and we'll go."

"No, you need to do it now! I know there's something wrong."

"Dorris, I would be endangering other men's lives, and I can't do that. Let's go get the kids, bring 'em here, and you guys spend the night."

As Walter finishes, Jonathan walks up and asks, "Ya'll okay?"

Walter looks at Jonathan with a concerned expression and says, "Jonathan, go to Dorris and Elmer's, pick-up the family, and bring them back here."

Dorris hollers, "No, I'll go get them!"

"It's okay, Ma'am. It won't take me long. I'll be back in a jiff, and besides, I have to pick up my car anyway," responds Jonathan as he heads toward the house.

"Can I take your horse?"

"Let 'em go Dorris; it won't be long."

"Okay, okay."

As Jonathan rides up to the house, the kids come running out, "Where's Mom?" they shout.

"She told me to get ya'll; you're staying at the Livingstons' tonight."

"What about Papa?" asks Clyde.

"I don't know. I'm just doing what I'm told."

Sara thinks, *How wonderful this is! Maybe I'll get to play the Livingstons' piano.*

Chapter 9

The Search

As morning dawns a new day, there's still no sign of Elmer. Walter gathers the hired hands and goes over the details of the search. He divides the search party into two groups and leaves a couple of hands at home to man the fort. A few concerned church folk straggle in just in time to divide up and hear the instructions.

Walter announces, "We have two teams, one will head north while the other heads southeast. We really have no idea where he is. It takes two days to go around the property without fixing any fence. He may be stranded or hurt; so leave no stone unturned. Each party will take a wagon along for supplies and shelter, if needed. I don't see any new storms coming, but you never know about this valley. Listen up! You riders on horseback, ride ahead of the wagon, so the wagon doesn't slow down the search. One more thing, no matter what, be back here no later than tomorrow night. There's a marker halfway around the property. When you reach it, turn back and come home. Any questions? Then let's get riding!"

***

It's finally morning and Elmer's not feeling well. The chills are pretty consistent, he's exhausted, and at times he notices a shortness of breath. He thinks, *What more can go wrong?* With tears welling up in his eyes, he says to himself, "I lost my best friend, got caught in a snow storm, and broke my leg. I tore my hands up on barbed wire, lost my hat, got bit by a wolf, and now I'm coming down with one hell of a cold." Lying there he prays, "Lord, please send someone today to find me: I'm really in a fix. Thanks for staying with me and helping me through this. I look forward to what You're going to do through all of this. Amen."

***

It's toward mid-morning and the snow's still pretty deep in spots. Piled up in drifts as high as five feet in places, it definitely makes for slow going. While the wagons struggle, the men on horseback move along at a good pace. All either party sees are some stray animals. The party going north runs across some fixed fence lines, indicating Elmer's been through there. The party moving south, then north, takes notice of places where the fence line is still down; thus realizing Elmer has not gotten that far yet.

***

Mom tries to keep herself busy at the Livingstons' by helping Maggie with a pile of sewing that needs to be done. *If the circumstances were different, this would be fun*, Mom thinks. She could get used to sewing with Maggie's Singer sewing machine. Clyde's outside running around like most nine-year-old boys do. He strays toward his weakness, the horse corrals. Ruthie's enjoying a good book, and Sara's having a great time playing on the Livingstons' piano. She isn't very good, but she continues to practice. From the other room, Mom's going crazy as she listens to Sara miss note after note. Finally, she's had enough, so she gets up, walks to the parlor and sits next to Sara on the piano bench. She wraps her arm around her and softly says, "It's not that one; it's this one," pointing to the "G" key.

Sara turns her head to the left, looks at Mom, and asks, "How do you know?"

"Just try it, go ahead!" Mom confidently replies.

Turning back to the keyboard, Sara plays the stanza again, and sure enough, the song sounds the way it should.

She looks at Mom and asks, "How'd you know?"

"I used to play a piano a lot like this one."

"Really?" Sara responds in amazement.

"Yes, really," Mom answers, with a smile.

She continues, "Growing up in Indiana, our family had a piano, and I took lessons religiously. But that was a long time ago."

"Oh, Mama, please play something for me, please, please?"

★★★

Little Clyde makes his way over to the horse corral, where two beautiful Palominos stand. As he gets closer, they both become spooked and one steps back, while the other runs to the other end of the corral. Clyde notices how much they look alike with their gold coats and white manes and tails. They both still have their bridles on, so he thinks, "Must be from being walked this morning." Clyde approaches the corral fence, puts his left foot up on the first log, and climbs to the top. He reaches over and tries to lure the horse that's still close with no success. Looking around, he sees a carrot on the ground next to a bale of hay. Jumping down, Clyde grabs it and climbs back on the fence. Leaning over, he offers the carrot with his left hand. The horse freezes for a second, and then takes a couple of steps toward the carrot. As the horse cautiously walks up to the fence, his focus is on the carrot while Clyde reaches for the reins with his right hand. As the horse takes the carrot, he grabs the reins and, with one fluid motion, leaps onto his back. He loves to ride, but Dad only allows him to get on his horse, Sacred—and only when he's around. Clyde thinks, *Boy, this feels great! I wish Dad could see me now.*

The horse begins to move and startles Clyde, who hadn't thought of what he'd do once he got on, so he grabs the reins and holds on tight. He flashes back to something Dad had taught him, *Pinch your legs around the horse's midsection.* That thought comes to him about the same time the horse realizes that Clyde is on his back. He starts out at a slow, steady trot. Clyde smiles and sits high in the saddle without a saddle, enjoying every minute of it. The more comfortable he becomes, the braver he is as he holds the reins in his right hand, takes his hat off with the left, and waves it in the air with a loud, continuous shout. A hired hand just inside the barn hears the commotion and comes running to see what it's all about. Spotting Clyde on the horse, he jumps onto the fence to watch the show. There's little he can do, especially now. The horse begins to buck and Clyde's face doesn't even show any concern. He's having the ride of his life, hollering the whole time, thinking, *Boy, it seems like I've been on him forever.* Then it hits him, *How do I get off?*

It doesn't take the horse long to show him the way off. With one mighty buck, Clyde understands the meaning of the law of gravity: "What goes up must come down." He falls on his right side with a loud thud. The hired hand, with a smile on his face, jumps the fence, grabs the horse's reins, and leads him away from Clyde. Clyde lies there in a panic. It's hard to breathe and he thinks, *I'm going to die! Come on, breathe . . . breathe.* He finally catches his breath and scrambles away from the horse. Once he's able to catch his breath, he gasps, "Wow, wow, wow, that was fun!"

"What are ya doing?" barked the hired hand. "Ya trying to get yourself killed?"

"Wow, that was great! Can I do it again?"

"No! Stay off the horses!" He yells, although after watching Clyde, he thinks, *Hey this kid has pretty good form for being so small.*

***

Mom's hesitant to play the piano; after all, it's been a long time. Sara says, "Mom, I'll get you my sheet music so you can play some songs." But Mom says, "That's okay, I don't read music."

"Then how do you play?"

"I hear the song in my head, and then I sit down and play it."

With a look of shock on her face, Sara says, "I've never seen anyone do that before. Come on, Mom, please play!"

After a moment of hesitation, the frustration of the day seems to fade as Mom adjusts herself on the piano bench. She places her hands just over the keyboard, and, remembering a song from childhood, begins to play. From the first note, she grins from ear to ear; Sara can tell she's having a great time. Partway through, Mom starts to sing and the rest join in. Sara turns to see Walter and Maggie walking into the parlor, singing as loudly as they can. *They look as though they're having fun, too*, Sara thinks. Mom's face turns a little red as she tilts her head down in embarrassment, but continues to play.

When she finishes, Maggie comments in amazement, "Dorris, I never knew you could play! Where's the music?"

"Oh, I play mostly by ear."

"Really?"

"Yes, it's just something the Lord has blessed me with," she softly replies.

"If I sing a song, can you play it?"

"I can try!"

Right on cue, Maggie begins to sing the words to "I'm a Yankee Doodle Dandy." It doesn't take Dorris long to pick out the tune. They all stand in amazement, singing as Dorris continues to play without a hitch. Ruthie hears the music, puts her book down and walks into the parlor. Like everyone else, she stands there flabbergasted. Clyde hears the music as he runs toward the house. He flings open the front door and runs in, still pretty wet from falling off the horse into the snow. As he steps into the parlor, Ruthie nods at him in bewilderment and asks, "Did you know Mom plays the piano?"

Clyde bellows, "Mom, what cha doin' play'n the piano?"

Smiling, Mom turns to answer, then immediately stops playing. Her smile turns to a frown as she hollers, "Clyde! You're a mess! What happened to you?"

"Nothin'."

"What do you mean, 'nothing'?" Mom inquires.

"Nothin'."

"How did you get so wet and muddy?"

"Fell off a horse."

"What? What horse, when, where?" Mom shrieks as she gets up from the piano bench and moves toward Clyde.

"The one outside! It was so much fun, Mom. I wish Dad could have seen me!"

With that, everyone looks around and comes back to reality.

***

The search party to the north reaches the halfway marker and has only seen traces of Elmer being there. They contemplate continuing, but remember Walter's instructions, "There's a marker halfway around the property. When you reach it, turn back and come home." They hope the other party has found Elmer.

Meanwhile, the other search party plods along. It's getting close to turn-around time, but they're determined to reach the halfway marker. They stop to rest the horses, and while sitting on the back of the wagon, one of the men notices something just ahead.

He tries to focus, then lifts his arm, points, and says, "What's that over there?"

As they turn, he continues, "It looks like . . . oh no!"

The group quickly walks over to the object and, sure enough, it's Elmer's horse Sacred lying dead in the snow. They immediately realize Elmer's in trouble . . . without transportation he couldn't have gotten far. The saddle blanket's gone, along with pieces of the leather bridal. They scan their immediate surroundings for any signs of him. Finding nothing, they decide to spread out and walk in different directions. One walks along the fence, and after a short distance, waves his arms and hollers, "Hey, over here! Looks like someone's been here!"

The others stop in their tracks and scamper over to see what he found. Pointing, he says, "Look, on the fence; there's a piece of . . . looks like a glove, and it's got dried blood on it. Let's keep walking." As they walk along they see more small pieces of fabric, either clothing or gloves, imbedded in the barbed wire and know they have to be getting closer. Jonathan suggests, "Let's go back, get the horses, and meander up the fence line."

They sprint back, mount up, and continue the search. After riding a bit, they notice a pool of blood on the snow. Jonathan gets off his horse and finds a carcass spread out.

***

Elmer's freezing, shivering, coughing, and praying for this nightmare to end.

He says to himself, "When will they come?" Then hearing something, he says, "What's that?" Being as still as he can, he squints to listen as though that helps him to hear. Sure enough, voices—human voices! What a sweet sound! He begins to holler, but realizes his voice is gone. Every time he attempts to scream, nothing comes out. He thinks, *What should I do now?*

Jonathan identifies the remains, "It's a wolf. Elmer's still out here somewhere." Scanning the area, one of them says, "What's that mound over there?"

As they walk over to check it out, another says, "Listen, what's that?" The men stop in their tracks and listen for any little sound.

Reaching the mound, someone says, "Hey, it looks like Elmer's Stetson. He must be close!"

"There's that noise again. Can ya hear it?"

"Yeah, sounds like someone pounding."

As they pan the area for signs of life, one remarks, "Shouldn't there be a shed somewhere close by?"

"That's right; it should be over this way," another points toward a bank of snow.

He runs over and listens. "The sound's coming from under here somewhere." They frantically begin to dig and soon uncover part of the shed. The more they reveal, the louder the pounding. Finally, they expose the door, give it a tug, and it swings open. The stench from inside about knocks them out. They aren't sure if he's dead or alive.

Jonathan bends over and hollers, "Elmer, you alive?"

When there's no response, he hollers again, "You alive?"

Elmer tries to talk, but is only able to make a squeaky whisper. The rescuers all hear it and let out a cheer. They've found Elmer and he's alive!

Jonathan turns to one of the men and instructs, "Ride back to the wagon; tell 'em we found him and hurry!"

It's a short ride. The wagon's already past Sacred and just a short distance away when the rider meets them. It's getting late, and they need to start for home or they won't make it back before dark. Helping Elmer from the shed, Jonathan makes a quick evaluation. He's really pale, his eyes are bloodshot, and overall he doesn't look good. Being trapped for two days in close quarters hasn't done much for the aroma, either. The combination of sweat, urine, and other unmentionables makes for a horrid stench. Elmer closes his eyes. Knowing the brightness of the day will blind him until they adjust, it takes a while before he looks up at the guys who normally work for him. Barely able to speak, he whispers in a raspy voice with tears in his eyes, "Boy, I am happy to see you guys!"

Jonathan reassures him, "You'll be fine, we'll get you back to the ranch house."

"Thanks, Jonathan."

Chapter 10

The Rescue

Mom pushes away from the piano and commands Clyde, "Follow me!" Walking out of the parlor with Clyde in tow she says, "You should consider yourself lucky, young man. If your dad was here, he'd give you the strap, and you wouldn't sit down for a week."

"Ah, Ma, I didn't hurt anything!"

"That doesn't matter. You didn't listen to your Dad or me and for that you need a good old fashioned butt-whipping!"

Clyde prays to himself, *Oh, please let somethin' happen so I don't get a whoop'n.*

Taking a left out of the parlor and down the hall, she stops about halfway as she hears the sound of horses and faint voices. Dorris pauses, and then walks slowly toward the front door as she tries to make out who it is.

Clyde thinks, *Thank You, God!*

Mom arrives at the front door as the others scurry out of the parlor. As Walter opens the door and steps out on the porch, he sees six riders with a wagon heading toward the house. He can tell this is the search party that went north and shouts to the hands, "Did ya find him?" The first rider gallops up to the house and asks, "Excuse me, sir?"

"I asked if ya had any luck."

"Nope, but we found plenty of evidence that he'd been to the halfway marker, though."

"Like what?" Walter inquires.

"Well, the fence looks great. It's been repaired in a number of places."

"Okay, thanks. Go ahead and get the horses taken care of, and then get yourselves warmed up."

"Thanks, Mr. L." Looking at Dorris apologetically, he says, "Sorry Ma'am, but I'm sure the other guys have him."

***

The second team waits with Elmer for the wagon to catch up. Once it does, they make a soft place for him with the blankets they have. Then they lift him up into the back and cover him to keep him warm. He resists lying down because his body is sore and stiff from being in that position for the past two days. The shivers don't stop, even though the new blankets they brought are quite comforting. He wants to wrap up in as many as he can. As he does, he thinks, *Sitting up feels wonderful and just breathing fresh air is heavenly.*

He says a quick prayer, "Thank You, God, for bringing these men to find me. Please bless each one of them." Elmer notices that each time he tries to take a deep breath, he begins to cough. Not just once or twice, but it takes awhile before he stops. "Oh well, at least I'm saved. Things are definitely looking up." Jonathan rides in the back with Elmer and fills him in on how the family's doing and how worried they are about him.

Jonathan asks, "What happened?"

Elmer explains all he can, though his voice is about gone. He tells him about the tree limb, Sacred, the crawling, the raccoon, and the wolves.

Jonathan sits there amazed and thinks, *I can't believe what this man has gone through!* Every once in a while Jonathan has to lean forward to catch what Elmer is saying. The noise of the wagon, along with Elmer's fading voice, makes it hard to hear. Now just over an hour away from the ranch house, sunlight is rapidly fading.

Too Old, Too Fast

***

Turning to walk back into the house, Mom begins to cry. Clyde looks up at her, wraps his arms around her and whispers, "They'll find him!" She gives him a big squeeze and walks into the parlor with everyone else. Clyde runs to the back of the house to change clothes, thinking, *I don't want Mom to remember what she was about to do before the men came back.*

Maggie says, "Is anyone hungry? I'm going to get supper going."

Dorris responds, "I'll help you, Maggie," as they walk into the kitchen. Maggie walks over to their new Kelvinator refrigerator and pulls out some leftovers to heat up. As Dorris sets the table, the conversation turns toward their future.

Dorris begins, "Elmer and I have always had a dream of owning our own place. You know, something we can call ours."

"That's a great dream." Maggie responds, "Walter and I would like to help you fulfill those dreams."

Dorris gently replies, "You know, we do appreciate that, but we don't want to be beholden to anyone."

"Oh, that's not it at all. We consider you our family. You know, not having our own and all," Maggie assures Dorris.

"Well, we consider you two part of our family, too, but we still can't take advantage of your generosity."

"Tell you what. When Elmer gets back we'll all sit down and talk about it. We love you guys," Maggie says, wrapping up the conversation.

Dorris doesn't respond, thinking, *There's really nothing to discuss, our minds are made up. Well, at least mine is.*

As the sun slowly sets, the sky is once again brilliant with colors. This would be a beautiful sunset if not overshadowed by the fact that there are still no answers. Maggie and Dorris set the food on the table and, as everyone gathers around, Dorris thinks, *This is going to make me crazy, another day about gone and no news. Elmer where are you?* she screams to herself.

Walter stands at his familiar spot at the head of the table and gives thanks for the meal, "Lord, You know our hearts are troubled, and we lift up Elmer and the search party to You. Please protect them and get them home safely. Bless this food and thank You for the hands that have prepared it, in Your Son's precious name, Amen." As he closes in prayer, you can hear riders off in the distance rapidly approaching the house.

***

It won't be long now; in fact, in the twilight you can see the silhouette of the ranch house in the distance. Elmer struggles to stay awake. Jonathan reaches over and touches his forehead, which is burning with fever.

"We're almost there, Elmer, and we'll get ya taken care of."

"Thanks, Jonathan," Elmer weakly responds.

Jonathan motions to one of the riders to come over and tells him, "Let's switch. You ride in the wagon and I'll head to town to fetch the doctor." He hollers at the riders in front, "Ya'll ride ahead. Tell the family and have them prepare a place for Elmer."

Hearing the horses coming, they all glance around the room at each other. Dorris moves first, making a beeline to the front door with the others close behind. She thinks, *They have to have found him! There's no place else to look. I hope he's all right.* Reaching the front door and swinging it open, she sees one of the riders jump from his horse and head to the porch. Stepping out onto the porch, Walter asks, "Any news?"

"Yes, sir, we have him. He's in the wagon and should be here any minute."

"Is he all right?" Dorris asks.

"A little beaten up from the ordeal, but he's alive."

"Praise God!" shouts Mom.

"Jonathan headed to town to fetch the doc; should be here soon."

"Doctor? I thought you said he was okay!"

"He is, I think, but has a busted-up leg and looks pretty weak. Jonathan just wants to play it safe."

Jonathan rides into town, thinking, *It'll be shorter and faster if I ride from where they are instead of going all the way back*

91

to the ranch house. As he enters town, he runs into a couple of friends who encourage him to grab a drink with them. He replies, "I will as soon as I take care of something." Arriving at the doc's office, he pounds on the door. When there's no response, he pounds again. Still no response.

An elderly lady walks by and says, "Doc's not there, saw him leave a short bit ago."

"Where'd he go?"

"Not sure."

"When's he coming back?"

"Not sure."

"Boy, you're no help!" Jonathan says sarcastically.

"Thanks, I guess! Just wanted to let you know!" the lady says, returning the sarcasm.

Jonathan walks away, shaking his head and thinking to himself, *Boy, she's a lot of help. What should I do now?* He no more finishes the thought when his buddies find him again and try to persuade him to get a drink with them.

"Come on, Whiskey, just one little drink. What's it gonna hurt?"

"Okay, okay, I'll I check back in a minute or two," he replies.

***

The wagon pulls up in front of the house and Dorris goes a runnin'. Looking in the back of the wagon, she sees Elmer curled up in blankets, gives him a quick once over, and notices his right leg is stiff and straight. He looks terrible, shivering, pale, and coughing.

"Hurry, get him in the house!" she demands.

She wonders, *Should we take him to the hospital? No, that's too far, must be over twenty miles. Besides, Jonathan's getting the doctor.*

Mr. L walks up as the men lift the litter with Elmer and instructs them, "Follow me, we'll take him upstairs." He turns and walks toward the house as the four cowboys follow close behind, being careful not to bump his broken leg. Clyde holds the door open and, as they walk by, he can't believe how bad he looks. The girls stand in the doorway of the parlor, and Clyde gives them a look of concern, and says, "Did ya see 'im and how white he looks? Hope he's going to be okay."

Sara walks up to Clyde, puts her hand on his shoulder and answers, "Don't worry. Mom's going to take care of him just like she takes care of us, and we all get better."

"Yeah," Ruthie says, "Dad's in good hands. Besides, didn't you hear? Jonathan went for the doctor." Before she can finish, Clyde shoots out the door and heads to the wagon.

Ruthie looks at Sara and asks, "Where's he going?"

"Don't know," Sara responds.

Once inside, the cowboys follow Maggie up the staircase to the second room on the left and gently place him on the bed. Dorris follows close behind.

She turns, and says, "Thank you so much for finding him and getting him home to us. Now, if you would, please give us some privacy so I can take care of my man."

"You're welcome, Ma'am. We'll be just outside if ya need us," one of them responds.

As Clyde reaches the wagon and looks around, the cowboy sitting in the wagon asks, "What cha lookin' for, boy?"

"I'm lookin' for my dad's horse, Sacred. Ya seen him?"

The cowboy climbs down, and says, "Come here, boy."

Clyde walks over as the cowboy squats down to his level. He looks him in the eyes, takes off his hat, holds it against his chest and nervously rolls the brim. "Boy, your pop's horse gave his all."

"What's that mean, Mister?"

"Well, on the way in, your pop told the story how this here horse of his saved his life."

"Okay, but where's Sacred?"

"Listen up little guy. Ya ever hear the song, 'A Cowboy's Best Friend Is His Pony?'"

"Yeah. So?"

"Well there's a line in there that says, 'When we ride on the ranges in heaven.'"

With that, Clyde gets a funny look and says, "Ya mean he's gone to heaven?"

"Yeah, little man, he laid down his life fer your pop. He saved his life."

Tears well up in Clyde's eyes, as he protests, "No, not Sacred! Pop loved that horse; he was part of the family." The cowboy reaches over and tousles Clyde's hair, "It's okay there partner; it's goin' to be all right." Clyde bursts into tears and runs into the house. As he passes Sara and Ruthie, they ask, "What's wrong with you?" Clyde stops long enough to tell them that Sacred's dead. Ruthie asks, "Who told you that?"

Clyde replies, "That cowboy by the wagon!"

The girls walk out to get the full story about Sacred. They too break into tears when they hear how Sacred saved Dad's life.

★★★

Whiskey, having a few drinks with his buddies, gets pretty wrapped-up in conversation. They reminisce and laugh about the stupid things they've done while drunk. One drink leads to another, then another, and pretty soon he forgets why he came to town, and doesn't realize that a couple of minutes after he left the doctor's office, Dr. Albright returned.

★★★

Elmer opens his eyes and can barely speak, but still manages to get out, "I must be in heaven. An angel is standing over me."

With tears in her eyes, Dorris responds, "Oh, you be quiet now and let me take care of you."

Clyde hits the top of the stairs and heads toward Dad's room. One of the cowboys grabs him and asks, "Whoa there, little guy, where ya headed?"

"To see my dad."

"It's probably not a good time. Just wait here with us."

"Well . . ." Clyde answers as he ponders his next move. Unable to stand still, he rocks back and forth and rolls his eyes. As the cowboy turns his head, Clyde takes the opportunity to bolt past him into the room. "Dad, is it true Sacred's dead?" Clyde asks.

Mom quickly turns, takes hold of Clyde's arm, and directs him to the door, "Not now, Clyde!"

He pleads, "But Mom, I hear Sacred's dead!"

"Clyde, now's not the time. Please go."

"Okay, can I at least hug him?"

"One hug and then out you go. He needs his rest."

Clyde charges over to the bed and gets his hug and then glances back as he turns to walk out and says, "Dad, I love ya," grinning from ear to ear. Mom escorts him to the door and notices the girls standing there watching.

She asks, "Want to see Dad?"

"Sure!" they both say with smiles on their faces.

As the girls go into the room, Maggie walks up.

Clyde says, "Dad doesn't look too good. Is he going to die?"

Maggie, with a gentle motherly look on her face replies, "Oh, Clyde, don't talk like that! He's going to be fine; he's just had a couple of bad days. Let's pray for him right now. 'Lord, thank You for getting Elmer home safely. We ask that You be with him and heal him from the hurts he has. Amen.'"

Clyde hollers, "Amen!" and takes off back toward the room. Maggie asks, "Where're you going?"

"I'm going to see my Dad, 'cause we just prayed for God to heal him, and I want to see it happen."

"Clyde, it doesn't work like that!" Maggie shouts back, but it's too late. He's already opened the door and gone back into the room. He's not in there long when Mom once again escorts him out, along with the girls, and says, "Now, you guys go downstairs. I'll come and get you when you can come back up."

Clyde takes off down the stairs looking for Maggie. He finds her in the parlor crocheting and says, "You need to pray again."

"Why's that, Clyde?" she asks.

"'Cause it didn't work the first time," he says, frowning.

Dorris asks for warm water and more blankets. Elmer's a mess. She's going to have to take his clothes off and bathe him here in the room. She starts by working on his hands. They're all cut up and covered with dried blood, almost every inch of them. She's tries to be extra careful with the cuts, but that's impossible to do because there are so many. Once she finishes with his hands, she takes off the rest of his clothes. Walter knocks on the door and Dorris says, "Enter." He pokes his head in and says, "I have some night clothes here, if you need 'em."

"Thanks, that'll be great," Dorris softly replies.

Walter walks in, places them on the foot of the bed and turns to leave. Dorris looks up and says, "Thank you, Walter, for all you've done for us and for sending the men out to find Elmer. Have you heard from the doctor yet?"

Walter turns to respond and, seeing the big alligator tears in Dorris' eyes, says, "We love you guys and will do anything for you. I will go to town myself and check on the doctor."

Mom once again turns her attention to Dad. In no time she has his clothes off, examines his leg and cleans him up. The shivers have subsided somewhat, and he's beginning to settle down. Now she turns her attention to trying to get his temperature down. She thinks, *This cough sounds horrible! I sure hope the doc gets here soon.*

Walter walks down the stairs and into the parlor, looks at Maggie, and says, "Something must be wrong in town. I'm going in to check and find out why Doc's not here yet." He walks over and gives her a kiss, as he always does before he leaves. Then he speeds away in his year-old Ford.

It doesn't take long to get to town, and he heads straight to the doctor's home. He knocks firmly on the door and a middle-aged man answers, "Walter, what can I do for you? Everything okay at the house?"

Walter responds with a look of bewilderment on his face, "Evening, Charles." He thinks, *How could you still be here, knowing what happened to Elmer?*

"Ya haven't heard?"

"Heard what?"

"Haven't ya seen Jonathan?"

"Not tonight."

Walter tells Doc that they need him at the ranch. Charles grabs his coat, hurries to the car, and they speed back to the ranch. On the way, he tells Doc all he knows about what happened. Passing through town, Walter notices Jonathan's horse and thinks, *I wonder what happened? Why didn't Jonathan bring Doc to the ranch? I'll have to get to the bottom of this, but first I have to get Doc to the ranch.*

***

After a while, one of the guys with Whiskey asks, "Where ya been the last couple of days?" This triggers Whiskey's memory and he screams, "Oh, my God!" He stumbles to his feet, runs to the door, glances off the door post and falls into the street. He shakes his head, stumbles back to his feet, staggers to Doc's office and again bangs on the door. Doc's neighbor hears the ruckus and comes out to tell him Doc left with someone in a car. He immediately thinks, *Who picked up Doc? Had to be Mr. L. Boy, if it was, I'm in deep trouble. Oh well, not much I can do now. I need another drink!*

***

Arriving at the house, Doc heads directly upstairs. Dorris and Maggie are sitting with Elmer as Doc enters the room. He asks them to leave and the first thing he examines is the leg. He asks Elmer who had set it for him, and Elmer explains the story. Doc Albright listens intently and explains that the leg has been perfectly set. "The only thing I need to do is set you in a cast, but that won't be for a couple of days." Doc asks Elmer where the scrape marks on his leg came from. He explains about the run-in with the wolves and begins to cough uncontrollably. Doc Albright takes note and asks, "How long you had that cough?"

Once his cough is under control, Elmer answers, "The last couple days." Doc continues to ask questions and Elmer answers the best he can. Finally, he tells him, "Try to get some rest." Doc walks down to the parlor where everyone's sitting, looks over at Dorris and says, "We need to talk."

Chapter 11

I Love You My Man

Walter drops Doc off at the house and heads back to town to look for Jonathan. He goes over and over in his mind what he's going to say when he finds him. As he pulls into town, he spots Jonathan's horse, parks down the street, and begins walking around town looking for him. Unable to find him, he recalls, *His nickname is Whiskey. I wonder if the rumors are true. Well, I'll check the tavern to see if he's there.*

As he passes by its big picture window he glances in and, sure enough, Jonathan sits at a table in the corner, roaring with laughter. Walter walks through the big double doors just as Jonathan looks up and sees the displeasure on his face. He stands the best he can as Walter walks to the table. Sticking out his right hand to greet Walter, he says, "Evening sir, just passing some time with my friends till Doc gets back."

With a look of disgust, Walter replies, "Jonathan, I picked Doc up about an hour ago and took him to the ranch. What are you thinking? We have a man out there that's at death's door! You come here to get Doc, and I find you drinking!"

"I can explain, Sir," he slurs in response.

"I don't need your explanation! You lied to the misses and me and then you do this? You're done, pick up your pay tomorrow; you're fired!"

Jonathan sways as he asks, "What cha mean, 'I'm fired?'"

Walter pulls out his wallet as he repeats, "Just what I said, you're fired!"

He pulls out some bills, hands them to Whiskey, and declares, "Here's your final pay. I don't ever want to see you again." Walter turns to walk out, but Jonathan, in an attempt to save some face in front of his friends, fires off some words too crude to repeat. He closes his tirade by saying, "Fine, if that's the way you want it. I'll get even; just wait and see!"

***

Doc sits next to Dorris and explains his diagnosis and recommendations for Elmer as Walter walks into the parlor and stands behind Dorris. Dr. Albright explains, "The leg's fine, it'll heal, and as far as I can tell Elmer's doing okay. However, there are three things that concern me: the wolf bites, the bad cough, and the fever. The wolf bites are pretty superficial, but it may have had rabies. It takes a while for any symptoms to show, so I recommend that we get some vaccine and begin treatments right away."

Hanging onto every word, Dorris responds, "Whatever you think is best, Doc."

He continues, "He can't take deep breaths without coughing, which means his lungs are pretty congested; and with the fever, it could mean pneumonia."

"What do we do for that?"

Doc instructs, "All you can do is keep him comfortable and try to keep the fever down. I just gave him some medicine, and I'll check back in the morning. Can't do much more tonight, so Walter, if you'll kindly take me home?"

"Sure Doc, glad to."

"Thank you so much, Doc. We'll see you in the morning," Dorris says.

Too Old, Too Fast

As evening sets in, the kids are clearly glad to have Dad around; they all want to sit with him in his room. Mom feels pretty uncomfortable being at the Livingstons' and wishes they were at home.

She thinks, *Elmer will be better by morning and we can move him then. The only thing that matters now is that the family's back together.* Elmer seems weak, speaks in a whisper, and has a difficult time breathing and getting comfortable. Mom whispers, "You all need to get ready for bed and start heading that way." One by one, the kids walk over to Dad's bed and kiss him good-night.

Clyde turns to go, looks back at Dad and says, "Don't forget about our trip, just you and me, right?" Elmer nods his head, winks and gives Clyde a big smile. He sure looks forward to spending that time with his son.

For now, though, he thinks, *Things don't quite seem right. I feel horrible and have these chills every now and again.* He fades in and out of consciousness as his mind drifts to thoughts about heaven and what it will be like. He knows some scriptures about it, but he still has numerous questions. Pastor Red will have the answers if he can talk with him alone. This would be a great time with the kids getting ready for bed and all.

As Dorris sits next to the bed and talks to Elmer, she notices he no longer responds to her voice or makes any purposeful movements. His breathing has become pretty labored. She bends over in an attempt to waken him. Feeling his forehead, she realizes he's once again burning with fever, and she needs to get it down quickly. She runs out of the room to the top of the stairs and hollers for Maggie and Walter. Dorris figures he must be in a semi-coma from the fever. Maggie and Walter come running and enter the room right behind Dorris. As they enter, Elmer begins to convulse, which scares everyone to death. Walter immediately heads to the door and shouts back, "I'm going for the Doc." Elmer, still in his daydream state, listens intently to some soft beautiful music. He can't quite catch where it's coming from, but it's sure wonderful.

C. E. Andrews

***

Walter drives faster than he ever has. Arriving at Doc's, he jumps out, runs to the door, and begins pounding. The lights come on one at a time as Walter stands there waiting for what seems like hours, but it is actually only seconds. Finally, the knob turns and the door slowly opens. Doc sees Walter, and says, "It must be Elmer!"

"Yeah, Doc, please hurry!"

Walter hurries back to his car to wait. It doesn't take Doc long to grab his black bag, run out of the house, and jump into the car.

"As you drive, fill me in."

Walter explains and when he finishes, Doc shakes his head. With a sad face, he says, "I was afraid this would happen."

"What's that mean?"

"Well, you know, Elmer wasn't in the best shape when I got there, and I didn't want to alarm anyone."

"Yeah? And? Listen Doc, shoot from the hip and tell me what's happening!"

"Well, I don't think he's going to make it."

"What?" Walter screams.

Doc tries to be calm, "The only other time I've seen a man this bad, he didn't make it. You see, he not only has all the injuries, but he also has pneumonia and the body can only fight off so much. With the fever the way it is, the only thing that can save him is a special healing from God."

***

Dorris frantically sponges his forehead and neck with cool water to get the fever to break. The children hear Mom holler and the ensuing commotion and come to the room to see what's going on. She's having no luck getting the fever down, and with the possibility of another convulsion, she looks at Maggie and asks, "Can you please take the kids downstairs?"

As Maggie rounds them up, they voice their displeasure. Mom turns and gives them a look only a mom can give, which they quickly recognize and reluctantly obey. As they head downstairs and walk into the parlor, Clyde sees Walter and Doc come through the front door and notices the look of concern on Dr. Albright's face as they walk by. Doc enters the room and observes Elmer's labored breathing. Getting his stethoscope out of the bag, he can hear the crackle with each breath.

Mom looks up at Doc with tears in her eyes, and says, "Doc, please do something, please!" Doc walks over and places his stethoscope on Elmer's chest. It's what he was afraid of, crackling, from fluid in his lungs. Only now it's worse than it was a few hours back and getting worse with each passing moment. He turns to Dorris, looks into her eyes and says, "There's nothing more we can do for him now; he's in the hands of the Lord." With this, Dorris breaks down and sobs uncontrollably. Maggie walks up and embraces her as Dorris collapses into her arms. They walk out of the room into the hallway.

Doc looks at Walter and asks, "Do we want to call Red?"

"I'll fetch him," Walter replies.

Doc walks out into the hall, and in between sobs, Dorris asks, "How long does he have?"

Trying to be kind, Doc softly replies, "Not long, you may want to let the children come in and say their good-byes."

With this, Dorris once again weeps bitterly. A couple of minutes pass before Dorris realizes she needs to pull herself together, for the sake of the children. She looks in on Elmer who has a peaceful look on his face.

She responds to Doc, "We'll wait for Red to get here; he'll know how to tell the children."

***

Walter retrieves Red and heads back to the ranch. Along the way, he fills him in on all that's taken place. As they pull up and walk toward the house, Red's mind's running a hundred miles an hour and his stomach's not far behind. He thinks, *What am I going to say to the family? What will I say to Elmer? Lord, I'm not very good at this, but I want to be Your servant. Please give me words that are comforting.* Walking up the staircase to the bedroom, he notices Dorris standing outside in the hall with Maggie and Doc. She looks up and walks toward him, her eyes swollen and red from crying. After shaking his hand she says, "I need some help telling the children," pausing to gain her composure, she continues, "that Elmer's going to die. Will you help, please?"

Doc looks at them and says, "I'll help too, if you want."

"Thanks, Doc," Red quickly responds.

They head downstairs to the parlor as Doc asks, "You want me to tell the children about his condition?"

Dorris, having a hard time already, nods her head in agreement. As they walk through the open doorway of the parlor, the kids are sitting on the floor playing Old Maid.

Doc begins by saying, "Hey kids, we have something to share with you."

"Is it about Dad?" asks Ruthie.

"Yes, as a matter of fact, it is."

"Mom, what's going on?" Sara begs for an answer.

"Listen to Doc; we're trying to tell you," Mom responds

Doc interjects, "Ruthie, kids, we have done all we can right now for him."

Sara jumps in, "Dad doesn't look or sound too good."

Red speaks up, "Kids, your dad has had a rough couple of days, and with being cold and all, it has affected his health. Like Doc said, he's done all he can. At this point Dad's not responding, and Doc doesn't think he's going to make it."

"Wait a minute, what does 'not going to make it' mean?" asks Sara as tears begin to pool in her eyes.

"Well, it means your dad may be going home to be with his Lord."

"You mean he's going to die?!" exclaims Ruthie.

"Dad's going to die?" screams Clyde, "No, he can't! We haven't gone on our trip together, and he promised."

"Yes, his only hope is for the Lord to step in and heal him," Red softly replies.

"Well, I know God is going to do something, 'cause Mrs. Livingston and I prayed for God to heal Dad!" Clyde hollers as he heads up to Dad's room. They all quickly follow. Red and the others stay outside in the hall, while Mom and the kids walk into the room. Elmer stirs and tries to focus his eyes, but has a difficult time. Mom walks up, holds his hand, and tells the children to stand on either side of the bed. As the kids walk to his side, Dad puts on a smile. With that, Mom lets go of his hand and the kids each grab onto one. They squeeze tight and tell him how much they love him and can't wait for him to come home. The three older kids bend over, give him a kiss, and walk out of the room crying. Rachel, the youngest, sits on the edge of the bed. She crawls up to Dad and gives him a big hug and smile that warms his heart as nothing else can.

Dad gives her a kiss and, with a weak voice, asks to see Red. Dorris calls for Red and he walks into the room, looks at Elmer and asks, "You want to speak alone?"

Elmer weakly nods his head.

Red looks at Dorris and says, "Elmer and I have some things to discuss. Please leave us alone for a couple of minutes." Dorris picks up Rachel and walks out.

As the door closes, Elmer can only get out a couple words at a time and asks, "Dying?"

"Yes, Elmer, there is nothing more the doctor can do."

Elmer puts his head back, closes his eyes and says, "Heaven?"

Red replies, "Yes, Elmer, if you have placed your trust in Jesus Christ, you will be with Him in heaven today."

Elmer forces out, "Like?" Red can barely understand, but answers, "It's a wonderful place; it's where God dwells. Scripture tells us, 'Blessed are those who die in the Lord henceforth, Blessed indeed, says the Spirit that they may rest from their labors, for their deeds follow them!'"

Upon hearing this, Elmer smiles.

Red continues, "Elmer, you have nothing to fear in death. Romans 8:38-39 says, 'For I am persuaded, that neither death, nor life, nor angels, nor principalities, nor powers, nor things present, nor things to come, Nor height, nor depth, nor any other creature, shall be able to separate us from the love of God, which is in Christ Jesus our Lord.'" (KJV)

Again Elmer smiles and uses one word to describe what he's thinking, "Family?" With that his eyes tear up and he begins to cough.

Red assures him they'll be taken care of.

Elmer raises one finger to indicate one last request and whispers, "Dorris." Red walks to the door and says "Dorris, your man wants to see you."

By this time, his breathing is very shallow. Dorris walks up, grabs his hand, bends over, and kisses him on the forehead, "I love you, my man."

He reaches up, caresses her cheek and wipes the tears from her face. With his eyes tearing as well, and with all he has in him, he takes two short breaths and whispers in a low tone, "I love you, my bride." He attempts to take a deep breath, but it only causes him to cough again. Gasping for air, he can breathe no more. Dorris breaks down and leans on the bed as she weeps. Doc walks in, checks for vitals and finds none. "I'm so sorry, Dorris."

Chapter 12

Omen?

It's early morning long before sunrise as Dorris opens the door and shuffles into the hallway. She looks up at Maggie, barely able to speak as tears stream down her face, and whispers, "He's gone."

Maggie chokes up as she walks up to Dorris, who lays her head on Maggie's shoulder and sobs. Maggie says, "Oh Dorris, we'll get through this together. Let's go downstairs now and allow Doc to do what he needs to." Maggie leads Dorris down into the parlor, where Clyde and Rachel have fallen asleep on the floor. Ruthie and Sara sit in a daze, unable to sleep. Their eyes are red and swollen from crying. Mom sits down across from the girls and places her head in her hands.

Ruthie looks at Mom and asks, "Is he gone?"

Maggie interjects, "Yes, Ruthie."

With the news, the girls break down and cry as they walk over to Mom and fall at her feet. Leaning against her legs, they put their heads on her lap, and she runs her fingers through their hair. It's silent for what seems to be forever. Their hearts are broken; their minds are empty, and emotions endless.

Sara asks Mom, "What'll happen to us now?"

"We'll be fine," Mom responds.

Maggie again interjects, "Yes, Mr. L and I are going to take care of you guys. After all, we're family."

Mom counters with, "Thanks, Maggie, but we'll be fine. We just need to get through the next few days."

Maggie quickly backs off, "Of course, of course! Let's get through this, and we'll deal with the other things later."

The sky lightens as a new day is ushered in. With each passing moment, the sun reveals more of the morning sky. It's a three dimensional view with layers of colors that you can almost reach out and touch. The colors are offset by dark clouds, almost as if it too is mourning and not looking forward to the day. In town, rumors are already making their way around, and since it is such a small town, it doesn't take long for the news to spread.

***

In room six of the local boarding house, a knock comes to the door and Whiskey slithers to his feet to answer it. He has a horrible hangover from the night before and can't imagine who'd wake him up at this hour. Opening the door, he sees one of his drinking buddies. "What do you want at this ungodly hour?" Whiskey asks as he walks back and flops on his bed.

"Just thought ya might want to know."

"Know what?"

"Elmer Lewis died last night."

"What? Ya sure?" Whiskey asks in surprise.

"Yeah, I'm sure. Don't know all the details, but rumor has it he passed away sometime early mornin'."

"Oh, my god, what've I done?"

"What' cha mean by that?"

"I was supposed to fetch the doc, but instead I went drinking with you guys. Oh, my god."

"Don't blame yourself. Ya didn't do nothin'."

"Thanks! See ya later." Jonathan retorts as he slams the door. "Wow, I can't believe it," he says to himself as he paces around the room, holding his still throbbing head. "How could I have been so stupid? People are going to hate me when they find out what I did—all for a drink. What am I goin' to do?"

Too Old, Too Fast

***

Saturday morning, the day of Elmer's funeral, the family's busy trying to catch up on chores. With Dad gone, they have twice as much to do, so Mom waits until the last minute before she calls them in to get ready.

"Is Pastor Red doing the services, Mom?" asks Ruthie.

"Yes, dear; they'll be the first services in the new church building."

"Who do you think will be there?" Sara asks.

"I don't know, but Dad knew a lot of people so I imagine it'll be quite full."

Clyde responds, "We'd better get there so we can get a good seat."

Mom bends down and answers, "Sweetie, we'll have good seats. They'll save the front row for us." Tears trickle down her face.

A short time later, a knock comes to the front door. Ruthie walks over and jerks on it until it opens to discover Mr. L standing there. He looks at Ruthie and says, "We'll have to get that door fixed. You all about ready?"

"We'll be with you in a moment, Walter," Dorris responds.

"Okay, Dorris, I'll wait outside for ya."

Walter walks back toward the car as Clyde follows close behind. About halfway to the car, Mom hollers, "Clyde, come back in here." When he reaches the door he looks up to see the old horseshoe Dad would always slap as he walked into the house. Clyde imitates what Dad would do; he spits on his hand, rubs them together, and jumps as high as he can in an attempt to slap the old horseshoe. Unfortunately, he's far too short or 'too short in the britches' as Dad would have said. He just whiffs into thin air. Walter chuckles at his effort, then walks over and asks, "Want some help?"

"Sure!" Clyde responds with a grin.

Walter reaches down, picks him up by the waist and raises him high enough to slap the old horseshoe, and slap it he does. In fact, so hard he hollers, "Ouch!"

As Walter sets him down, he warns, "Better take it easy, Clyde, you don't want to hurt yourself."

"I'll do it on my own one day," Clyde boasts.

"Yes you will, Clyde; yes you will."

Mom hollers, "Clyde, hurry up and get your hair combed."

As Clyde runs back in, the rest of the family walks out, ready to go.

"Better get a move on," Walter says.

***

The church is beautifully decorated for the funeral with flowers everywhere. The new coat of white paint sets off the stained glass window at end of the building. Final touches had been completed the day before, so everything is fresh and new.

As Red wraps up his funeral preparations, his wife comes in, gives him a kiss and says, "Know that I'm praying for you. It's exciting to know that so many people will be here—some who have never been in church before. I pray the message makes an impact on their lives."

"Thanks, Honey."

An hour before the service begins, people are already gathering to check out the church, their first opportunity to see the finished product. Red greets the people as they arrive and prays to himself, "Lord, I hope we can hold everyone." It's impossible to move it outside, as the rain's been falling at a steady pace since midmorning. The gravesite will be a mess if it keeps up.

The family members arrive and are escorted into the church straight to the front row just like Mom said. Music plays softly in the background as people walk about greeting each other. Red walks out, and for the first time, stands in the pulpit of his new church and begins.

"On behalf of Dorris, Ruthie, Sara, Clyde, and Rachel I thank you for coming today. I would like to read a couple of scriptures." He opens his Bible and reads from Psalm 147:3-5 and Proverbs 3:5-6. Psalm 147:3, 5 says, "He healeth the broken in heart, and bindeth up their wounds. Great is our Lord, and of great power: his understanding is infinite" (KJV) In Proverbs 3:5-6, we read, "Trust in the Lord with all thine heart; and lean not unto thine own understanding. In all thy ways acknowledge him, and he shall direct thy paths." (KJV)

Red asks everyone to please bow their heads, and prays, "Loving Father, almighty God, we come to Thee in this hour because we are in need of Your comfort and we realize that only through faith in Your Son can we have victory over the grave. Grant each one the faith to see beyond these dark hours. We ask for thy grace to give strength to these troubled hearts and to lift burdens from these weary minds. In Christ's precious name! Amen."

Jonathan sneaks into the back of the church and glances around, looking to see who's there. The place is packed. It's been a long time since he's been in a church and he's hoping the new building won't fall down. He looks toward the front and sees Ruthie with the family. He notices Sara looking back at him and then leaning over to say something to Ruthie. He thinks, *They must be glad to see me*, and smiles.

The pianist plays Elmer's favorite song, "Red River Valley," as Sara looks around and sees Jonathan standing in the back. She leans over to Ruthie and whispers, "What's he doing here and what's he smiling about?"

"He worked with Dad; why shouldn't he be here?"

"'Cause he's the one who caused Dad to die!"

"You don't know that."

"Do too."

Mom hears the whispering and glances over and places her finger against her lips to tell them to hush.

"How?" Ruthie whispers.

"Overheard Mr. L and Red talking yesterday. Mr. L fired Jonathan because he didn't bring Doc to the house. He got drunk instead."

"I don't believe you."

"Well, it's the truth! I'll prove it to you later."

Mom tersely whispers, "You two show a little respect, or you're in big trouble."

After the song, Red continues his tribute to Elmer.

"On May 26 1892, in Eastern Kansas, there was born a little baby boy to Roy and Ellie Lewis, and they named him Elmer. He grew up in a poor family working the fields. Elmer and his younger brother worked right alongside their parents. At the age of sixteen, he left home and worked numerous jobs just to get by. On July 4,1912, he married Dorris Shewmaker. They have four children; Ruthie, Sara, Clyde, and Rachel.

Red continues, "Elmer's family was the apple of his eye, and he loved them not only with his words, but most of all with his actions. He would spend time with them playing cards, board games, and singing. Dorris was truly the love of his life."

Red looks down at Dorris as she lowers her head and begins to cry. Dorris doesn't look down for long and as she looks up, she mouths the words to Red, "Thank you." The children look at Mom as Ruthie puts her arm around her and whispers, "We love you, Mom." Dorris acknowledges her by laying her hand on her knee and giving a gentle squeeze.

Red continues, "Elmer always made me feel comfortable, and he will be missed. I can say that my life is richer for having known him." As Red speaks, Walter thinks, *Maggie and I have been blessed to have Elmer work for us. He was one of the hardest workers I have ever known. Our ranch wouldn't be what it is if he hadn't been here. Not sure what's going to happen now without him.* He quickly tunes back in to Red's message. "Death is the ultimate limitation all must face. It also brings the most frustration. We have questions like, 'Is there really a God? Is there such a thing as eternity? Does heaven really exist? Is there a hell? What is death like?'"

Whiskey listens intently to Red's words and thinks, *These questions make sense, never really thought about 'em before. How can I find the answers?* Tuning back in to Red, he hears the answers, but not what he wants to hear.

Red again opens his Bible and continues, "When looking for the answers to these questions, there's only one place to turn, one place to trust, and that's the Creator's own words. They're found only in His Word, the Bible. Psalms 116:15 says,

"Precious in the sight of the Lord is the death of his saints." (KJV)

Precious because God sees death from His side; whereas, we only see it from this side, the mortal side. Our eyes only see the end, and our minds immediately think of loss. We have to remind ourselves of the great joy and happiness Elmer is experiencing. This may seem strange to us, to use words like these when speaking of death, but far from strange for those who have a personal relationship with Jesus Christ. Elmer left a greater heritage than we can ever imagine. It will only be as the years go by that you will become aware of just how great this heritage is."

Boy, is that the truth. Dorris thinks. *It will be years before the kids will understand what a great man their dad was.*

Red proceeds, "Remember, it says the death of a saint is precious to God. Think of the excitement God must have as He shows His children heaven for the first time. Can you imagine the thrill and excitement Elmer must have as his eyes behold what Jesus has prepared for him and all of those who have a personal relationship with God through Christ?"

Jonathan listens intently and can't believe that Red's making this more about this Jesus character, than about Elmer. His mind wanders, *Who is this Jesus anyway? Why would Red turn this into one huge sermon? This religious stuff is more than I can handle. I need to get out of here, but it'll be pretty obvious if I leave now. Oh well, I'll just "suffer for Jesus,"* he says under his breath with a chuckle.

Red's still preaching as Jonathan tunes back in, "The same Christ who stood to welcome Stephen into heaven (see Acts 7:55) will stand and welcome us. John (see Rev, 21:4) says that someday God will wipe away our tears. The same hands that stretched the heavens will touch our cheeks. The same hands that formed the mountains will caress our face. The same hands that curled in agony as the Roman spike cut through, will someday cup our face and brush away our tears forever. Elmer stepped out of this world into heaven. One moment in time all things changed. No more limitations of the old body; no more pain and illness. All this was replaced by a new body. Heaven is described as a place of no tears, pain, death, or fear. It is written in the Holy Bible in the Book of First Corinthians 2:9: 'But as it is written, Eye hath not seen, nor ear heard, neither have entered into the heart of man, the things which God hath prepared for them that love him.' (KJV) We will be in awe! Heaven is beyond our imagination. We cannot envision it. In our most creative moment, at our deepest thought, at our highest level, we still cannot fathom eternity. Anything we imagine is inadequate. No one has even come close, and no one ever will. It is beyond us."

About this time Mr. L looks around the church and sees faces that have never darkened the doors of the church. One in particular grabs his attention—Big Al, the owner of the tavern. Walter thinks, *Wow, what's he doing here? What kind of connection did he have with Elmer? Oh, he's probably here to be with the rest of the crowd, like most people on Sundays. Boy, this is pretty heavy-duty. Red's taking the opportunity to preach to those who may have never heard preaching before.* He prays for those in the crowd, and then catches Jonathan's eye and prays for his heart to be open to the truth.

Red moves on, "One of the pressing issues on people's minds during times like this is the reality of death. One day it will be me people are remembering, and the same can be said for each of you. As human beings, we don't like any kind of limitations placed on us. We like to think we're invincible, the masters of our own fate."

Jonathan agrees with this part, *That's right; I am the master of my own fate.* He thinks, *Who else is? I can do anything I want.*

By this time, Clyde's pretty fidgety and thinks, *If Dad were here, he'd ask, "What'cha got, ants in your pants?"* This brings a smile to his face. Dad had a lot of those sayings, "See you later, alligator; after a while, crocodile; in the afternoon, raccoon," all come back to his mind. *I sure hope this is over soon,* he thinks.

Red begins to wrap up the service, "But this isn't reality. We must realize that there are so many things beyond our control. We don't like it that way, but that's the way it is. It's that way with our health. That's why we must trust in the One who knows all and has a plan for our lives. This kind of trust involves letting go and knowing God will catch ya. None of us have long to live. In our brief span of years, God graciously allows us breath in our lungs, a heart that beats over a hundred thousand times a day, and sufficient mental and physical strength to carry on. The primary purpose for our lives is not to be used for ourselves, but pure and simple, it is to bring glory to His name. And Elmer did that very well. Faith in Jesus means trusting the plan He has for our lives. It doesn't mean understanding that plan; it means believing God knows best for us. I want to close with this portion of scripture found in the Gospel of John 3:15-21: 'That whosoever believeth in him should not perish, but have eternal life. For God so loved the world, that he gave his only begotten Son, that whosoever believeth in him should not perish, but have everlasting life. For God sent not his Son into the world to condemn the world; but that the world through him might be saved. He that believeth on him is not condemned: but he that believeth not is condemned already, because he hath not believed in the name of the only begotten Son of God. And this is the condemnation, that light is come into the world, and men loved darkness rather than light, because their deeds were evil. For every one that doeth evil hateth the light, neither cometh to the light, lest his deeds should be reproved. But he that doeth truth cometh to the light, that his deeds may be made manifest, that they are wrought in God.'" (KJV)

After Red closes in prayer; his wife walks over, hugs Dorris and gives her condolences, and then hugs the rest of the family. The others line up to give their condolences to the family as Red and his wife walk to the double doors in the back of the church and stand there to wait for the family to go to the graveside. Red's wife leans over and whispers, "Our first service in our church was a funeral. I sure hope that's not a bad omen!"

***

As Red prays, Jonathan sneaks out. This religious stuff is more than he can handle; he needs a drink and heads to the tavern. About halfway there, the others begin to file out of the church. At the families' request, the graveside service is going to be private, so not many will be going. Everyone's invited to the Livingstons' for a meal afterwards.

***

Just before he steps into the tavern, Jonathan hears someone call his name. He turns around to see Mr. L and thinks, *What does he want?*

Mr. L hurries his steps and asks, "Can we speak for a moment?"

"Guess so; just don't know what more needs to be said."

"Well, Jonathan, I just want to ask ya to forgive me for the way I talked to ya the other night."

"What?"

"Yeah, I wasn't very kind with what I said and all. Will ya forgive me?"

"Why should I? Ya said some hurtful things, and I won't forget them."

"That's your choice. I just want ya to know I don't hold these things against you.

"Well, you shouldn't! I didn't do nothin' wrong."

With that, Mr. L can tell he's getting nowhere and says his good-byes.

"One last thing, Mr. L," Jonathan says.

"What's that?"

"Do I get my job back?"

"No, Jonathan, I can't do that."

"Then all this was just a front to make you feel better. Fine! I didn't want it back anyway. Remember what ya said, 'I never want to see ya again!' Well, right back at ya." Jonathan turns and walks into the tavern.

Mr. L stands there, speechless, and thinks, *Not much more I can do.*

Chapter 13

There's a New Horse in Town!

he graveside services are short. As they conclude, sunrays beam through the clouds, and the rain stops as though the weeping is over. Walter opens the car doors, acting as their chauffer, and the family slides in. As they pull away from the cemetery and head to the ranch, Clyde turns around in his seat and whispers to himself, "Good-bye, Dad. I'm goin' to miss ya."

It's a quick drive to the ranch and a number of people have already arrived for the gathering. Dorris frowns and thinks, *This is going to be hard.* Walter stops in front of the house and Dorris steps out and opens the door for the kids, "On your best behavior. Understand?"

"Yes, Ma'am," they acknowledge.

She walks along with Rachel on her hip, shaking hands and hugging those she knows as Walter escorts them into the house. Ruthie and Sara are busy talking to and getting hugs from some people they barely know, while Clyde, off in his own little world, thinks; *I'll probably never get to fish or hunt again.* He desperately misses Dad and doesn't quite know what to think about all that's going on. He grabs some food and decides to go outside and enjoy the sun.

From a distance, Pastor Red watches Clyde head outside and wonders, *Is he all right? He sure looks lost.*" Not wanting to be pushy, he waits a while before he goes looking for him. Clyde's nowhere in sight until Red turns the corner by the barn, where he spots him kicking up dirt. He ambles up from behind, and asks, "Hey Clyde, how you doing? Want to talk?"

"Nah," Clyde responds.

"You must have some questions that need answering. How 'bout it?"

Clyde takes a moment to think, kicks the dirt, looks up, and tearfully asks, "Why didn't God heal my dad? Ya know, if He's really so great and powerful . . . why?"

Red, taken aback by the question, stands there not knowing what to say. It never dawned on him that a nine year old could come up with a question like that.

Looking for the right words to say, he responds, "Well, Clyde, we just have to trust that God knows what He's doing."

"How do you do that? All I know is I'll never be able to fish or hunt with him again. Does God really hate me that much?"

"Whoa there, cowboy. Hold on a minute; there's more to it than that!" exclaims Red.

"Oh, yeah! Like what?"

"Clyde, there are some things someone your age just can't understand, and I believe this is one of them. Even we as grownups have a hard time with it."

Clyde shakes his head in disbelief and thinks, *If a pastor can't even answer my questions, then there must not be any answers*. He replies, "There it is again, either my age or my size! That's great. I'm not old enough to ride a horse and not old enough to understand this. Well, I guess there really isn't a God if ya ain't got no answers."

Red tries to make the best of it, "Don't be so quick to judge! Come on; let's go back to the house." Clyde watches Red turn and head back to the house. He stops after a few feet and asks, "You coming?"

Clyde responds, "Nah, I'm goin' over to the corral."

Too Old, Too Fast

On the way back to the house, Red's mind races, *I didn't do a very good job of reassuring that young man, but what more could I have said? Not sure, I've had some of the same questions at times in my life, and I've just trusted. But why? I guess I need to find out.*

***

Ruthie and Sara stand just inside the parlor, which is packed with people talking and eating. Sara notices Ruthie scanning the room, and asks, "Who ya looking for?"

"No one."

"Yeah, ya are! You're not looking for 'im, are ya?"

"None of your business!"

"Ruthie, ya know what I told ya!"

"I don't believe you!"

"What do ya mean, ya don't believe me? Why would I lie to ya? I'm your sister!"

"I don't think you would intentionally lie to me, but I think you misunderstood what they said."

"Ruthie, I don't trust the guy. There's just something 'bout him. Please be careful!"

Ruthie sees the concern in her sister's eyes and replies, "I promise I will."

***

Clyde walks over to the corral and climbs up a couple rails. He reflects back to the last time he did this. *What a great ride, that was so much fun! One day I'll be riding horses all day. How great will that be?* Standing on the second rail, he hears someone walk up behind him. Not wanting to turn around, he thinks, *It's probably the pastor again with something to say about God.*

He feels a hand on his back, and a gentle voice asks, "How ya doin', Clyde?"

Clyde recognizes Mr. L's voice, and he turns around to look. He can tell Mr. L's been crying; his eyes are red and puffy. It seems that's all everyone's been doing lately.

Sniffling, Clyde answers, "Guess I'm doing okay. Really don't know how I should be doing! Things don't make sense in my head. Don't really know what ta think anymore."

Tilting his head, Mr. L replies, "It's been a tough couple of days for ya, but all of us are going to work through it." Tears trickle down Clyde's cheeks as he says, "I just know it's gonna be hard going home tonight without Dad being there," he turns and looks into the corral to hide his tears.

"I know, Clyde, but I have something that may make it a little easier."

Clyde jerks around, almost falls off the fence, and asks, "Like what, Mr. L?"

"Well Clyde, it's something from your dad and me. We were saving it to surprise ya for your birthday, but I think your dad would want me to give it to ya now."

"A gift from Dad and you? How's that possible with Dad dead?"

"Yeah, I know, but we've been planning this for a long time."

"Wow, what is it, Mr. L? Oh please tell me, please!"

"Okay, turn around."

"Ya want me to close my eyes or something?"

"No, that's okay, just look straight ahead."

"Okay, so what?"

"What do ya see?

"Three horses."

"Well, one of them is yours!"

"What? Really? Which one?"

"You see the little colt?

"Yeah, the black and white one?"

"That's the one. Let me tell ya the story behind him. Your dad and I talked about Sacred and what a great horse he was, and we thought how great it would be for him to have an offspring."

"Offspring?"

"Yeah, ya know, a little horse that he would be the daddy to."

"Oh, okay."

"Well, your dad and I allowed Sacred to mate with one of my mares and that's the colt over there. Clyde, he's all yours. He'll have to stay here until he gets a little older, but he's all yours."

"He's mine? I can name him and everything?"

"You sure can!"

"Oh, boy, when can I ride him?"

"Well, not so fast. We have a lot of work to do to train him. Let's name him first."

"Can I think about it?"

"Sure, take your time."

Clyde takes off running toward the house, stops and runs back, and says, "Thanks Mr. L; thanks a lot!"

"You're welcome, Clyde, you're very welcome." Mr. L smiles as Clyde takes off to the house and hollers back, "I can't wait to tell Mom!"

***

Ruthie's still looking for Jonathan and is surprised he hasn't come. She can't understand it. He's the one who found Dad, went to town to get Doc and had been close to him at the end. She thinks, *Why didn't he come? Are the rumors true?* She decides to walk outside; maybe he's there. As she opens the beautiful hand-carved front door and steps out on the porch, Mr. L steps up on the first step.

"Afternoon, Ruthie, how ya doin'?"

"As well as can be expected, I guess, Mr. L. Thank you for all you've done. I know Mom appreciates it, and so do I."

"You're welcome, young lady. Where ya headed?"

"Just came out to look for someone."

"Oh, yeah, who might that be? I'll let ya know if I've seen 'im."

"Well, I was thinking Jonathan might be out here."

"Nope, haven't seen him! Why would you be looking for him?"

"Well, I just wanted to say thanks for all he did while Dad was gone, and thank him for finding Dad."

"If I see 'im, I'll tell 'im."

"Thanks, Mr. L. See you later."

As the day winds down, the visitors gradually bid their good-byes. Big Al, the tavern owner, walks up to greet Dorris. She really doesn't like him, not because of him personally, but because of what he represents. She doesn't even know why he came. Elmer had no dealings with him as far as she was aware. He takes her hand and gives his condolences. Not realizing the food was brought by the people of the church, he says, "Ms. Dorris, I would like to assist in paying for this gathering. I know you need the help, and it would be my pleasure to provide it."

Dorris is surprised by the gesture, and before she thinks about it, she rudely replies, "Thanks for the offer, Al, but I wouldn't accept anything from you because I don't believe it's right how you make your money. So . . . thanks, but no thanks."

"Just trying to be neighborly, but I guess that ain't good enough fer ya. Good day, Ma'am." He tips his hat, turns, and walks out.

Clyde comes bursting through the back door of the house, hollering, "Mom, Mom where are ya? I got something to tell ya, Mom!"

As Al walks away, Dorris hears Clyde hollering. Her first thoughts are, *Oh Clyde, what have you gotten yourself into now*? Following his voice to the back of the house, she walks down the hall as Clyde comes sliding around the corner.

"Guess what, Mom?"

As Mom begins to respond, Clyde interrupts, "Bet cha can't guess what Mr. L just did. Come on, Mom, guess!"

"Clyde, if you'll slow down, I'll try. Let's see, he gave you a ride on a horse? No, that can't be it. He gave you a fishing rod?"

"No, Mom, much bigger than that."

"What do you mean *bigger*?"

"Mr. L gave me a horse! Can ya believe it? My own real horse!"

Mom warns him, "Clyde, don't tell a fib like that!"

Too Old, Too Fast

"Really, Mom, he gave me a little horse! Said that Dad and him were gonna' give 'im to me for my next birthday. He's offsprung, or something like that, of Sacred."

"You mean *offspring*?"

"Yeah, that's it!"

"Well, I'll have to talk to Mr. L about that."

"I'm so excited! Thanks, Mom."

Mom's not as excited. She thinks, *There they go again, doing things without even asking. Now how can I say no? I'm not looking for any handouts, and besides, how can I afford to feed another horse? We're probably going to have to get rid of the other animals as it is. Oh well, I'll take it one day at a time. But I will talk with Walter and Maggie.*

As Ruthie walks toward the barn, she sees someone standing in the shadows by the corral. She wonders, *Who can that be?* and cautiously approaches. As she gets closer, she can see it's Jonathan and asks, "Why are you out here? Come into the house."

"No, I think it's best if I stay here."

"I saw you at church, but when they closed in prayer you left. How come?"

"Yeah, I ain't much for funerals, reminds me of dyin'. Oh, I'm so sorry."

"That's okay, I'm kind of getting used to it, which is real scary."

"I ain't had anyone die I was close to before. Your dad was the first," Jonathan confides.

"For me, too."

"How ya doin' with it all?"

"Well, better than I thought. I think the hard part will be when everything gets back to normal."

"If ya ever need someone to talk to, just come a callin'."

"Thanks, Jonathan. I'd better get back now. See you later."

As Ruthie walks away, she glances back over her shoulder and waves. Jonathan waves back and thinks, *Wow, that's one great gal. She can make a blind man look twice. I'm definitely going to stay close to her. She'll need someone and I want to be that one. What a prize catch!*

C. E. Andrews

***

The Livingstons are such gracious hosts. As Dorris begins to clean up, they stop her in her tracks. Maggie grabs her hands, looks directly into her eyes and says, "You get your family together, and Walter will take you home."

Dorris answers, "I can't leave you with this mess."

Maggie replies, "Dorris, some of the ladies from the church are staying to help. Now you go on and take care of your family."

"If you're sure."

"I'm sure; now you go on."

Dorris gathers the kids out on the front porch. The sun is rapidly disappearing below the horizon as the family piles into the car, and Walter walks out of the house. Dorris looks up to see him carrying something. As he walks over to her door, he says, "Dorris, I have a couple of things of Elmer's I thought you would want."

She tears up as he hands them to her. It's Elmer's ten gallon Stetson and his black duster coat. She can just hear him say, *Yep, that there hat has helped me get many a drink for Sacred and myself.* It surely looks the part, well-worn, but Elmer's favorite. She smells the leather headband and pictures Elmer walking in the house and trying to toss it on the top of the coat rack. The duster, a full-length black canvas, is still dirty from Elmer's ordeal. She thanks Walter and thinks, *What am I going to do with this stuff? I'll probably just throw it away.*

On the way home, it dawns on her that Elmer had a steamer chest where he kept important items. She concludes that's where the hat and coat will go. Driving up to the house just doesn't seem right, and Dorris dreads walking into their lonely cottage. The kids look at each other and then at Mom for reassurance. Wanting to be a source of encouragement and strength, she says, "Oh, it's so nice to be home!" and gives the kids a big smile. They pile out of the car and thank Walter for the ride home.

Before he drives away, he says, "I'll check in on ya tomorrow, if ya don't mind."

"Thanks again for all you've done. Please don't put yourself out for us."

He responds, "See ya tomorrow."

As she opens the front door and walks into the house, Mom's stomach gets a big knot in it, but it doesn't take Clyde long to bring smiles to their faces. As he walks up to the door, he goes through Dad's routine of trying to hit the horseshoe (the spit, the rub, the jump), but once again falls short. The girls laugh, and Clyde says, "One day I'll do it; ya just watch and see." With a big grin, Ruthie messes his hair and says, "Yes, you will, little man, yes you will."

Once inside, Mom tries to get things back to normal as quickly as possible. She scoots the kids off to get ready for bed and heads into the kitchen. After a bit, she notices the hat and coat on the table, walks over to pick them up and heads to her room. She pulls the chest from her closet. It's prettier than Dorris remembered, about 20 inches long and 10 inches wide and deep, constructed of wood with a two-tone finish. The front has hasps with two swing latches and two side lifting leather handles. As she opens it, Clyde walks into the room and asks, "What's that, Mom?"

It's your dad's steamer," she replies.

"What cha doin' with it?"

"Putting Dad's hat and coat in it."

"Why?"

Now, that's a great question. What is she saving them for? "I don't know; just thought it might be nice to have sometime later."

"Can I have 'em?"

"Why would you want the steamer?"

"I don't know—just something to remember Dad by, I guess."

Dorris and Clyde break into tears and Clyde says, "Mom, I never want to forget my dad."

Dorris thinks, *I've been so self focused, I haven't thought about the kids missing their dad. That needs to change immediately!*

She tells him, "Sure, you can have it. One day you may be able to wear this stuff yourself, or help someone else with it."

Wiping the tears from his eyes, Clyde responds, "Thanks, Mom. Can I take it now? I have the perfect place to put it."

"Sure, where's that?"

"Can't tell ya. It's a secret," Clyde replies as he grabs the small chest and heads out the door. "I'll be right back."

Clyde heads to the barn and goes straight to the tool shed, knowing it has a fake floor. Pulling up a loose board, he kneels down and digs out enough dirt to put the chest in, carefully wraps it in a small blanket and tucks it in the hole. Standing up, he thinks, *There, Dad's stuff's safe. I can always come out here and get it when I need to.*"

Chapter 14

Time Flies

It's hard to believe it's already been a year since Elmer's death. So many changes have taken place. Mom's picked up extra sewing to help make ends meet; the town's people have been so caring and helpful. Ruthie has matured into a beautiful young lady and a number of young men have an eye, actually both eyes, on her—especially Jonathan. Unfortunately, she has an eye for Jonathan as well. He's been by her side throughout this past year helping her deal with the loss of her dad.

Mom still doesn't trust him and is not too keen on the idea of her spending so much time with him. Walter does all he can to discourage it as well. Jonathan's not allowed out to the house, so they see each other in town and walk together whenever they can. Ruthie's influence on Jonathan hasn't changed him. She remembers Dad saying something like, "Ya can't pull people up who don't want to be pulled, but they can sure pull people down." Then he'd quote, "Bad company corrupts good morals." Jonathan still drinks and thinks he does a good job of hiding it from Ruthie, but every now and again she smells it on his breath. While he's up to no good, he found another job working south of town on a small ranch.

Clyde has certainly grown up over this period of time, too, not so much in stature, but in responsibility. Over this past year, he's taken over Dad's chores, along with his. Most days he doesn't make it to school, using the excuse, "Things need to be done around here, and I can't do both." For extra pay, he assists Mr. L whenever he can. Sara and Rachel have fallen into a regular pattern of going to school and helping around the house.

Mom's made the biggest adjustments. She's now the mom, the main breadwinner and the one trying to keep it all together. The economic times make it tough to make ends meet, not just for them but for everyone, including the Livingstons. They're barely hanging on to the ranch; in fact, they're taking in boarders to help pay expenses. Topping it off, there's a severe drought; most of the cattle are dying before they're able to get to market. The lack of water is devastating. In an attempt to save the ranch, they've converted a large portion of it to growing potatoes. The Department of Agriculture, through local meetings, the county fair, and tours by experts, encouraged local ranchers to diversify their land. Walter and Maggie jumped on board, and if they hadn't, all would be lost by now.

While life is hard in the local area, the scary part is, the entire country's in trouble. Stories abound of people starving and others going from millionaires one day to paupers the next. The town's busy with people traveling through looking for work and sharing their stories. It's hard to figure out which ones are real and which ones aren't. The bank closed a few months back and the banker, Mr. Cline, snapped under the pressure. One day he walked into the church, knelt at the altar and prayed. Then he stood, moved toward the double doors, pulled out his revolver and shot himself dead. What's going to happen next? It's really unbelievable.

Dorris is thankful for all they have. Thanks to the Livingstons, they have the food they need. In reality, the Livingstons are feeding half the town. Dorris realizes things are okay for now, but she knows it can't last forever. She's busy around the house, the girls are off to school, and who knows where Clyde is. He's Mom's helper, always off doing something to help make ends meet.

Too Old, Too Fast

One day as Mom was mending to bring in extra cash, she's about to sit down to sew when there's a knock at the door. She slowly walks to the door and opens it to see Walter and Maggie standing there. She thinks, *They seem to have aged so quickly; they look much older than just a year ago. It must be the pressures of the times.* She knows all about the stress to provide just for her own family. She can't imagine what the Livingstons are going through. Maggie's the first to speak, which is par for the course, "Morning, Dorris, do you have time to talk?"

"Sure, come on in. Would you like something to drink?"

"No, thanks," replies Walter. "Dorris," Walter continues, "You know this past year has been tough on all of us. We can't imagine what your family's gone through with the loss of Elmer, and then this economic depression an' all. Maggie and I . . ."

With that Maggie jumps in, "What Walter is trying to say is you're our family and we want to help you the best we can, but with times being so difficult, we need you to move to the main house with us."

Dorris is expressionless as she listens to Maggie.

"We can board more people here and we won't have a bunch of strangers parading around in our home."

Dorris stumbles over her words, "Wow, this is a surprise! I'm not sure how to respond. I won't get in your way of what you have to do. When do you want this to take place?"

"Well, as soon as possible. We have people waiting," Maggie replies.

Dorris can tell Walter's not keen on the idea. He contorts his face as Maggie speaks, as if he had pain somewhere.

"Well, I'll begin packing."

"Oh, we can help do that. Don't worry, we'll have guys down here to help as soon as ya let us know you're ready," Walter quickly answers.

Dorris says, "I think we'll be okay. Can I get back with ya tomorrow?"

"Sure, that's fine. Ya know, Dorris, we look forward to having ya guys with us," Maggie says.

C. E. Andrews

***

Clyde makes his way to the Livingstons', as he seems to do each day. He wants to see Warrior, the name he gave his horse. They have become quite a team and have gotten pretty close. Warrior sees Clyde walk up and makes his way to the end of the corral. Clyde's in the beginning stages of breaking him, and all the cowhands want to give him advice on how to do it. One of them, who Clyde doesn't particularly like, tells him, "The only way to break a horse is to show 'im who's boss. You gotta use force with 'im."

Another individual, named Harold, Clyde has bonded with since Dad's death. He's like an older brother, a big guy around 6 feet 1 inch tall who is well over 200 pounds, broad shouldered, with a slim waist. What impresses Clyde is how large and strong his hands are. His nickname for Clyde is *Half-pint*, since Clyde is so small. His advice is, "You don't have to beat 'im to get 'im to do what you want. Treat 'im kind and care for 'im. When ya do that, he'll be your companion forever." Clyde likes that advice.

This is a special day. Clyde plans to halter Warrior and walk him around the corral. While few use the rope halter anymore, it's one Clyde can afford. It's homemade, naturally, with Harold's help. Harold's always full of advice and eager to show Clyde all he knows. He's been a cowboy for some time now, working on ranches in Texas since the tender age of twelve. This depression drove him from Texas looking for work. Hooking up with the Livingstons has been a blessing. He enjoys sharing all the tales he's heard and teaching Clyde the tools of being a first-rate cowboy.

As Clyde approaches Warrior with the rope halter, he begins to get a little nervous and backs away from him. Once Clyde stops, Warrior stops. Harold stands outside the corral and gives Clyde step-by-step instructions. "Pull out a sugar cube from your back pocket and reach out your hand toward him. You know how he loves sugar." With that, Warrior inches toward

Clyde, who gives him the sugar cube once he's within reach. "Good, now scratch his head, like you always do, from his mane to his nose. That'll have a calming affect on him and besides, he enjoys it. Now, slowly take the halter and place it over his head and grab hold of the lead rope." Clyde completes the tasks flawlessly.

***

Mom's in shock. She thinks, *What are we to do? I'm not moving to the main house! I want our privacy, but how are we to do that?* She decides to walk into town to see what she can find. Along the way, she has an hour to think about her criteria for a new place. *It needs to be cheap; it has to have two bedrooms, and a larger kitchen would be nice. Oh, yeah, I'm going to find that! Sure!* Jonathan's leaving town as she arrives and stops to say, "Greetings, Mrs. Lewis!"

"Hello, Jonathan."

"What cha doin' in town, Ma'am?"

"I'm looking for a place to live."

"Ya moving?" Jonathan responds with a puzzled look on his face.

"Yes, the Livingstons need my place."

"Wow! Well, I need to get going. If I hear of something, I'll let ya know."

"Thanks, Jonathan," Dorris replies, as she thinks, *I don't really need or desire your help, thank you.*

Jonathan walks away, thinking, *This can be the opportunity I've been waiting for. If I find something, I may get on her good side. I need to think. I know, I'll talk with big Al, the owner of the hotel. He's got a couple of places, but I'll have to wheel-and-deal to make it affordable.*

Dorris heads to the office of a friend she's known since the family moved to town. Opening the glass door, she sees Carl behind his desk. He stands up, walks over, and greets her with a hug. "Hello, Dorris, how's everything?"

"Well, not going very well right now. I need a place to move the family."

"What? Thought you were at the Livingstons.'"

C. E. Andrews

While Dorris explains the situation, Jonathan's busy at work. He walks into the Western Drake hotel, what locals call the WD. This hotel is really out of place, built in the late 1800s by an insurance company expecting great growth in the area. It never really fulfilled their expectations. That's when Alberto Ricci, known in town as Big Al, bought the place. He moved from Chicago with big dreams and renamed it after an icon in Chicago, "The Drake." He figured to have the same type of hotel only in the West, but he didn't consider his clientele base. With family money he remodeled this beautiful three story hotel, putting a fireplace in every room, a huge dining room, that's offset by a bar of equal size.

Jonathan heads to an office just to the right of the dining hall. Without knocking, he walks into Big Al's office. Al looks up from his desk and harshly asks, "What do you want? Never mind, get out of my office," two bouncers move toward Jonathan.

Jonathan pleads, "I just need a minute of your time."

Al holds his hand up to stop the bouncers and says, "You got thirty seconds."

Jonathan quickly explains Dorris' situation, but before he can finish, Al interrupts and asks, "Yeah, so what's that got to do with me?"

Jonathan continues, "I thought you might allow the family to move into that small home you have, for a greatly reduced rate."

"Why would I do that? That woman doesn't like me, and besides that, what's in it for me?"

"Well, it'd be great publicity for your business. Ya know, helping a widow, especially one the town's people love."

"Who cares? All I care about is making money."

"Well, there's one other thing I almost forgot to tell ya. She has a beautiful daughter. If ya help, I may be able to persuade her to work in your place."

"She's a doll?

"Oh, yeah, a real doll!"

"You can get her to work here?"

"I'm sure of it! It may take some time. You may need to be patient."

"Patient, huh! I'll show you patience. You have six months of free rent, but if the daughter isn't working by that time, out they go."

"That sounds great! You won't be sorry."

Chapter 15

Mom Decides

As Dorris explains her situation to Carl, she can tell by his facial expressions that things are not going well. He answers her questions indirectly and seems to beat around the bush for some reason. Dorris listens as long as she can stand it, then states, "Carl, don't patronize me. Do you have a place available or not?"

"Dorris, I think you need to reexamine your position. Moving to the main house will be temporary until this economy turns around."

Dorris doesn't want to hear it. "Carl, I want you to understand something. We've been friends a long time and I appreciate your concern, but we're not moving in with the Livingstons. Understand? Now, do you have a place or not?"

"Well, Dorris, it's not as simple as that," Carl says apologetically.

"Carl!"

"Dorris, you have to understand. There's a lot of people unemployed right now who are barely making it. I can't just ask them to leave. We all have to work together."

Dorris slouches down in the chair in disbelief, thinking, *My family is soon to be out on the street and no one seems to care. The Livingstons may be our only option.* She reflects back to when Elmer was missing, *That was hard being in their home then, and to do it all the time without a place of our own? I can't do that! In fact, I won't do it no matter what. I'm no charity case!*

"Dorris, there is nothing I can do for you right now. I'm so sorry," Carl concludes.

Dorris rises to her feet and says, "That's okay, we'll make it. Have a great evening." She quickly turns and walks away, tears rolling down her cheeks. She doesn't want his sympathy or for him to see her cry.

"Okay, see you later. Stop by again when you're in town."

Dorris simply waves as she walks out.

The kids are out of school by the time Mom walks out of the office. Jonathan's headed there to check on Ruthie. Sara sees him coming, and her blood begins to boil. She doesn't trust him; it seems life is all about Jonathan. She thinks, *He doesn't do anything unless there's something in it for him, and it doesn't matter who it hurts. I guess he's really no different than most people. It just seems to be more obvious with him.* Sara's a deep thinker. She reflects on people she knows who seem to have personal agendas, especially now with everything being so upside down. You'd think people would pull together more to get through this, but the opposite is proving to be true. People seem to only be looking out for themselves. They spot Mom and run to give her a hug. Ruthie asks, "What are you doing in town?" Mom proceeds to explain the whole situation with the Livingstons and the talk with Carl and all.

Sara asks, "What are we going to do, Mom?"

"Not quite sure yet, but we know the Lord will work it out."

"Yeah, just like He did with Dad," Sara says sarcastically.

"That's enough, young lady! You don't talk about God like that." Sara knew she'd crossed the line and thinks, *If there is a God, He knows what I'm thinking anyway, so the only difference is that Mom doesn't want to hear it. There's another example of someone being selfish, but the Livingstons? This is a total shock.*

Ruthie repeats Sara's question, "What are we gonna do, Mom?" Jonathan walks up just as she finishes. "Greetings to the Lewis family! Did ya find a place yet, Mrs. Lewis?"

"How'd ya know what's going on?" Sara demands.

"Saw your Ma when she came into town, and she told me the whole story."

"We'll be fine!" Sara retorts.

"Sara, that's rude," Ruthie pipes in.

"Oh, that's okay, Missy. I take no offense to it."

Sara wishes, *Well, you should, you jerk.*

"No, I haven't yet, but we will," Mom proclaims.

"Well, I got some good news fer ya!" exclaims Jonathan.

"What's that?" Dorris inquires.

"I done found ya a place."

"What?"

"Yeah, if you'll want it."

"How much?" Dorris hesitantly responds.

"Well, I explained the situation to the owner, and he's willing to let ya stay there six months free."

"Free!"

"Yeah, free."

"Jonathan, we appreciate that, but we can't stay anywhere for free. We're no charity case, so if we can't pay, we'll pass."

"Mom!" exclaims Ruthie, "He's just trying to help!"

"Well now, Mrs. Lewis, if you want to pay, I'm sure he'd be glad to accept. What do ya think ya can pay?"

"How about $10 a month? That's half of the going rate, but that's all we can afford right now. I'll be happy to pay more when I can."

"Don't see that as a problem, Ma'am. I'll let ya know tomorrow."

***

Clyde holds on tightly to the lead rope and walks ahead of Warrior. As the rope becomes taut and Warrior just stands there, Clyde gently gives the rope a tug, trying to get him to move.

Warrior raises his head in protest and Clyde looks to Harold for help. Harold softly instructs, "Don't tug too hard. Walk back toward him and stroke his head again." Clyde takes note of everything Harold says and follows it to a tee.

Harold gently continues, "Take another cube of sugar and make sure he sees it in your hand. Now, walk away slowly while ya grip the rope tight." As Clyde walks away, Warrior begins to follow. The rope becomes tight again, but this time it doesn't seem to bother him. Clyde walks Warrior around the corral and grins from ear to ear.

Harold says, "Great job, Clyde. Now stop and give him the sugar and place your arm under his throat and hug his neck." Again Clyde listens carefully and follows Harold's instructions. He then removes the rope halter, walks over to the corral fence, and climbs out. He looks at Harold with a toothy grin and says, "We did it! Thanks for the help!"

"Ya did it, Half-pint. We'd better get a move on, though. Your mom's probably wondering where ya are."

★★★

As Jonathan walks away, he heads toward the Western Drake thinking, *Wow, this is working out great! She's even going to pay rent.* Then his craftiness takes over and he decides to do something he would later regret. He deceitfully thinks, *I know what I'll do. I'll tell Big Al she accepted the deal for six months. Then I'll collect the rent, pocket the $10, and they'll never know.* As Jonathan steps into Al's office, he looks up from his desk and rudely demands, "What do you want?"

Jonathan, looking somewhat confused, replies, "She agreed to the deal."

"You'd better be right about this. I don't like people playing games with me."

"Oh, this is going to work out great for both of us."

"I don't care about you, but it had better be profitable for me! Now get out of here, I'm busy!"

"See ya later!" replies Jonathan.

"Hope not," big Al blurts out.

Jonathan walks out thinking, *Wow, this guy's scary. I'd better be careful.*

***

As Mom and the girls walk home together, they take turns carrying Rachel. She's had a big day. Clyde's busy finishing up the chores when he sees the girls approaching. He runs out, grabs Rachel from Sara and puts her on his shoulders. Mom says, "We need to have a family talk. Let's go inside and sit down at the table."

As they walk through the front door, Clyde tells Rachel, "Spit on your hands! Good, now rub them together. Great! Now reach as high as ya can and try to hit the horseshoe."

Rachel reaches as high as she can, but barely touches the top of the doorway.

Clyde says, "Good job, almost got it." The family sits around the table as Mom brings Clyde up to date with the day's happenings. He can't believe it.

"Ya mean we're gonna move? What about our things? What about Warrior? Is he goin' with us?" Clyde has a thousand questions.

"Yes, Clyde, we'll be moving off the property."

"Why don't we move in with the Livingstons? That'd be perfect!"

"No, Clyde, we're not moving into the Livingstons' home. With Jonathan's help, we've already found another place."

"Jonathan?" Clyde responds as he wrinkles his nose. "I thought ya said not to trust 'im! I'm confused, Mom. Let's just move in with the Livingstons."

"Yeah, Mom, I'm confused too," Sara jumps in. "Ya tell us not to trust 'im and now ya do the opposite. Mom, I don't like 'im. There has ta be something in it for him."

"You two, knock it off!" Ruthie demands.

Sara angrily blurts out, "How can ya trust anything he does when he did what he did to Dad?"

"You better keep quiet. There's no proof, and Dad probably would have died anyway," Ruthie rebuts.

"Oh, sure! Says who? Jonathan?" Luckily, by this time they're standing across the table from each other. Clyde, trying to help calm the situation, says, "Come on, Mom. Let's move in with the Livingstons!"

"Alright, all of you listen to me. I'm still the mom and we'll do what I think is best for this family. Understood?"

They respond in unison, "Yes, Ma'am."

***

The Livingstons are in the parlor reading their favorite book together, the Bible, when the topic switches to the events going on around them. The depression's affecting everyone. There are long lines for food and jobs, and families are being torn apart. Survival is not just day to day; it's meal to meal and moment by moment in many cases. People are living on powdered milk, dried beans, and potatoes. They've heard stories of people fighting over a barrel of garbage, young boys and girls 8 to 16 leaving school to work in factories, canneries, mines, and farms to help support their families. This is the harsh reality of the times.

As they talk, it dawns on them that they have their own example right before their eyes in Clyde; he goes out each day looking to find work to help feed his family. They conclude that they need to continue to help all they can, no matter what the cost, even if it means losing the ranch. Walter looks at Maggie and says, "We must continue to help Dorris and the kids." Maggie wants to support him, but she also reminds him of the reality of the times. "I know, but for all of us to survive, we have to do what needs to be done."

"Yeah, you're right. Them moving up here is the right thing for all of us. Clyde can go back to school and help us around here, which in turn gives us another hand. He's a hard worker, ya know!"

"It'll be a blessing for all of us," Maggie responds. Now comfortable with their decision, they go back to their reading. A couple of minutes pass before there's a knock on the door.

Maggie looks at Walter in bewilderment, "You expecting someone?"

"No, how about you?" Walter asks.

Maggie shakes her head.

Walter stands and tells Maggie, "I'll get it." He opens the door and sees Dorris. "Dorris, what a pleasant surprise! Please come in."

"Thank you, Walter."

"Maggie's in the parlor."

"I'd like to talk to both of you, if I could, please."

"Sure." He walks her into the parlor, and upon seeing Dorris, Maggie stands, walks over and gives her a hug. "It's always good to see you. Please have a seat," Maggie says.

Not wasting any time, Dorris jumps right in, "I don't want to take a lot of your time, but I've been thinking about this morning's conversation."

"Great," Walter interjects, "Maggie and I were just discussing how great it's going to be when you guys move in. Clyde can help us, while at the same time going back to school. And . . ."

Dorris blurts out, "Excuse me, Walter. Before you go on, I think you need to hear what I have to say."

Walter looks confused and glances at Maggie as if to say, "Have I missed something?" He responds, "What do ya mean?"

"Well, what I mean is, we're not moving in."

"What? Why not? It's a perfect fit!" Maggie responds in surprise. "Dorris, for all of us to survive, we need to do this."

"Well, I appreciate that, but I don't think it's the best thing for us. We don't want to be a burden on anyone."

"You're not a burden! Dorris, you're our family, and we want to help all we can," Walter insists. "Right, Maggie? Tell her."

"Dorris, we truly want the family here with us. Please reconsider."

"I understand, but with the kids growing up so fast, I just don't see it working."

Walter, now pleading his case, asks, "Just give it a try, please. If it doesn't work, we'll make other arrangements."

Dorris acknowledges, "I've already made other arrangements."

"What?" Walter hollers. "Dorris, don't do this! It's a mistake!"

"I'm sorry you feel that way. We'll start moving immediately."

Maggie, the level-headed one, says, "So, you've made up your mind?"

"Yes, I'm afraid so, but I want to thank you for all you've done for us."

"Where you moving to, if you don't mind me asking?" Maggie questions.

"We're moving into town, into a place Jonathan helped find."

"Jonathan!" Walter shouts. Now he knows for certain this is not a good idea. "Now, Dorris, let's think this through. Don't go jumping into something."

"I've already agreed and negotiated the rent."

"Dorris, you can live here rent free! I don't trust this guy, Dorris. Please reconsider. I think he's a wolf in sheep's clothing," Walter firmly states.

"Again, I appreciate your concern, but we need our own place." With that, Dorris gets up and heads to the door. Just before leaving, she turns and says, "Again, we do appreciate all you've done, and we all love you both dearly. Thank you, from the bottom of our hearts."

Chapter 16

Times Are Hard

F ive months have passed. The family moved into a little house in town and they, like everyone else, struggle to make ends meet. The Livingstons continue to offer help to Dorris and the family, but her pride always seems to get in the way. The depression seems to be getting worse, not better. Stories abound about starving children in the Appalachians chewing on their hands, nearly drawing blood. How much longer will this go on? Unemployment has gone from 3 percent to 25 percent and 37 percent among all non-farm workers, and farmers are losing their farms as well. There's one figure floating around that a million people have lost their farms. These are really tough times.

***

Jonathan's worked his way into the good graces of Dorris, but Sara and Clyde still don't care for him. At the same time each month, he comes by to pick up the rent. Mom struggles to make the $10 rent, but is thankful it's no higher. There are times of second-guessing for Mom when she sees Clyde working so hard and thinks, *If we had moved in with Walter and Maggie he'd be in school now. I wish I had done that.* Clyde tries to work but, at the age of ten, few people will hire him even for a day. Mom's unsure what's going to happen if things don't change in a hurry. Jonathan walks down Main Street and Big Al, owner of the WD, heads right toward him, a man on a mission. Jonathan glances around for a place to hide because he knows what he wants, but Big Al has him in his sights and there's no escaping. He walks right up to Jonathan, nose to nose, and says, "We need to talk *now*!" Jonathan knows it's about Ruthie. He hasn't broached the subject of her working in the bar yet, and the six months are about up. Al grabs Jonathan's arm and heads down between the buildings.

Jonathan thinks, *This isn't good.*

★★★

The Livingstons are barely hanging on to the ranch. They're thankful for what they do have and are still helping others when they can. Regular visitors at Dorris' home, they seem to be closer to them now than at any other time. The old cottage where Elmer and Dorris lived is quite productive. Without its income, the Livingstons would have lost the ranch long ago. They rent out not just rooms, but literally floor space. You have to do all you can in these times.

Dorris and the kids don't eat meals regularly; they eat when food's available. If they're able to get one meal a day, they consider it a blessing. Now, that's not a full meal, just maybe some beans, potatoes, and powdered milk. Mom does all she can and explains regularly to the kids about their situation. As they sit around the house one evening, a knock comes to the door. Clyde jumps up to answer it and there stands Pastor Red with a bag in his hand.

"Evening, Clyde," Red says.

"Evening, Pastor. What ya got there?"

"Something for the family."

Pastor Red and his wife are faithful to help others within the community. It's amazing; he always seems to be at the right place at the right time. He and his wife have a good-sized garden and trade veggies for milk and other things. With the downturn in the economic system, the locals have turned to bartering. This has become the main means of getting what you need. In these times, it isn't about getting what you want, it's about praying for what you need. One of Mom's sayings she taught the family is, "Never buy anything you can use, only buy what you can't live without." Even doctors are paid with corn, potatoes, or other products.

Clyde invites Red in. As he enters, he glances around, and sure enough, their cupboards are bare. Dorris greets him with a hug and asks, "What brings you by our place?"

"Well, the misses and I have a request."

"What's that?"

"We need some work done around the church, and we're wondering if Clyde can give us a hand."

"Sure, that'll be fine."

"Before you say yes, there's a catch. We can't pay you in money, but if we can give you this bag of food. It would really help us out."

"Oh, Red, that's fine. We're here to help no matter what. When do you want him there?"

"Tomorrow or the next, whichever works for you."

Mom has a sneaky suspicion that this is just a front. They do need help, but Red also knows Mom doesn't accept charity. With that, she says, "He'll be there first thing in the morning. Thanks, Red."

"You're welcome," Red responds, moving toward the door.

"You guys have a great evening."

"You too, and thanks again," Mom says, closing the door. She knows Red doesn't need any help at the church. There isn't that much to do, but he asked, and she wants to make sure Clyde stays busy.

***

As Jonathan walks down the little alley between the buildings, his mind races, *Has he found out about the rent I've been collecting?*

Al pushes him up against the building and places his big burly forearm in the middle of Jonathan's chest. With the other hand, he grabs him by the hair and slams the back of his head against the wall. He's close enough to Jonathan's face that Al can smell the alcohol on his breath. Eye to eye and nose to nose, he demands, "What do you think you're doing? Did you really think you'd get away with this?"

"What? I don't know what you're talking about," Jonathan denies. He notices another big guy standing at the entrance of the alley. "What do you mean? I haven't done anything."

"You told me that if I gave this family free rent for six months, the young lady'd be working for me by the end of it. Well?"

Not knowing what to expect next, Jonathan goes into his excuse mode, "Well, it's a bit harder than I thought!"

"I don't want excuses; I want results." Tightening his grip on Jonathan's arm, he concludes, "If I don't get what you promised, you're not going to like what happens. Keep your end of the bargain, or else."

"Are you threatening me?" Jonathan says, without thinking.

Grabbing his face and pinching his cheeks together, Al says, "It's not a threat; it's a promise." Backing away, he gives Jonathan a little pat on the cheek and says, "I'm sure I'll see you later." With that, he turns and walks back down the alley toward the street.

Jonathan thinks, *Whoa, that was close! I sure hope he doesn't find out about the $10 a month I've been pocketing. Oh, well, I'll deal with that if it ever comes up.*

***

At the crack of dawn, Clyde heads to the church to help Red. Mom committed him for the day, and he's not too happy about it. He has no desire to be around the church or Red. The front of the church is pretty. With its bell tower and big front doors, it's one of the nicest buildings in town, but this is the first time he's been here since Dad's funeral. The local kids have told some weird stories about things happening in the church, but Clyde thinks, *They're dumb stories.*

Red walks out with a smile on his face; he always seems to have a smile. He puts his hand out to greet Clyde, and out of respect, Clyde shakes his hand. They then proceed down the center aisle to the back of the church. Red hands Clyde a bucket of water and asks him to scrub the floors. He always works hard and never complains about any work he can find, especially now, after eating that great meal last night. They ate better last night than they have for months; well, at least since leaving the ranch. Clyde grabs the brush, and on his knees, begins to scrub. Before Red walks away, he asks, "Haven't seen your family in church lately. What have you been up to?"

Clyde politely answers, "Just the normal things—trying to work to eat."

Red gets more personal, "How are you doing? I'm concerned about you. Is there anything I can do?"

"Been fine, Pastor. Just like I said; been trying to work to eat."

"You know, Clyde, God loves you and your family. We'd love to see you guys back at church. You know, the Scriptures tell us, 'That God loves us so much that He sent His Son, Jesus, to die as the penalty for our sins.' Did you know that?"

"Can't say that I did," Clyde responds, still on his knees. His mind races back to Dad. *Where is this Jesus, when I need Him? He let me down. If He loves me that much He wouldn't have let Dad die. Look at all the hurting people; this is what a loving God does to His people? Don't need Him.*

Clyde focuses back on what Red's saying. He missed part of it, but that doesn't matter, it's just religious stuff anyway.

Red continues, "Have you ever asked Jesus into your life, Clyde?"

"Can't recall, Pastor," he replies through gritted teeth.

"Would you like to do that now?"

"Don't believe I would."

"Why not? Do you know what's going to happen to you when you die if you haven't asked Jesus into your life?"

"Don't believe I do, Pastor, and with all due respect, Sir, I need to get this here job done for ya. So maybe we can talk 'bout this later?" Clyde retorts. He thinks, *I don't mind working, but this being preached at is just too much. I hope I don't have to hear this for the next two days.*

Red comes back with, "Well, there are some things more important than work, but I'll let you get back at it. We can talk later."

***

Jonathan's in a real predicament. He needs to talk to Ruthie and contemplates, *How am I going to get her to agree to work in the tavern? If she doesn't, the family will be out on their own, or worse, I'll be in deep trouble.* He needs to get her alone, so he hitches a ride on the running board of a friend's truck and heads to the other side of town. As luck would have it, there's Ruthie walking alone toward home. As they drive by, he jumps off and hollers a thank you to his buddy. His momentum carries him right into Ruthie.

"Hey, there! How's my little filly?" Jonathan greets Ruthie.

"Hi, Jonathan."

"Ya make me laugh! You're always so prim and proper."

"Don't start in on me, Jonathan."

"I'm sorry, but we have to talk."

"About what?"

"Hey now, listen. I know how hard it is for your family right now, and I'm doing all I can to help. You know, finding the place, getting the rent reduced and all. I even found ya a part-time job!"

"You did? That's great! Thank you so much. How much does it pay?"

"'Bout $5 a week."

"Wow, that'll really help! Oh, Jonathan, thank you so much. When can I start?

"As soon as you like."

"Well, I guess I should ask what I'll be doing."

With a little hesitation and a smirk on his face, Jonathan replies, "It's working in the WD."

"Which one, the hotel or the bar?"

146

"Well, mostly the bar."

"Can't do that. Mom will never allow it."

"Why does she have to know?"

"You want me to do this behind her back?"

"Why not? It's for the good of the family."

"Because I can't—not for any amount of money!"

Jonathan gets panicky. This isn't going the way he wants it to. He thinks, *I can't take no for an answer! I'll force her to do it, or better yet, I'll shame her into it.* He grabs her with both hands and pulls her close. Ruthie hasn't seen Jonathan like this before. She looks into his eyes and sees anger building.

Looking into her eyes, he can tell she's scared. He says, "With all I've done for you and your family! I stick my neck out for ya; I get you a place rent-free. I mean, almost, at $10 a month! I'm here every time you need me. Your Mom's working her butt off, trying to feed you guys. Now you have the opportunity to help out and you say no! Wow, what kind of gratitude is that? Ya know, I can understand ya not caring about what I've done, but not even caring 'bout the family? I would have never thought!"

"Jonathan, you don't understand! Mom would pop a cork."

He let go of her arms, "She doesn't have to know, Ruthie! Do this for the family! They need you! Don't let 'em down."

"What will I tell Mom?"

"Tell her you have a job watching kids or something. Once she sees the money, she'll be thankful. By the way, that's a lot of money. Hold some back or she'll get suspicious."

"Okay, I'll try, but if I don't like it, I'm quitting."

"Oh, that's fine. You can quit any time you want."

***

Clyde finishes up at the church and walks toward home. Within 100 yards he spots Sara, hollers at her, and takes off running to catch up. As they look down the street, they see Ruthie walking ahead of them and they holler at her, but a vehicle roars by and drowns out their screams. As it passes, they notice Jonathan riding on the running board. To catch up to Ruthie, they quicken their pace. They start to cross the street but stop when Jonathan jumps from the truck and runs up to Ruthie. Sara grabs Clyde's arm and says, "Stay here. I really don't want to walk with him. I just don't like him."

"Me, neither," Clyde agrees.

Clyde and Sara stand across the street and watch as Jonathan and Ruthie talk. At a point in the conversation, Ruthie seems very excited, so much so she gives Jonathan a hug. Sara looks over to Clyde in shock. They've never seen Ruthie so affectionate.

"That makes me sick!" Sara exclaims.

"Me, too!" Clyde retorts.

As they continue to talk, things seem to sour as Ruthie shakes her head. About that time, Jonathan grabs her by the arms, and being very animated, talks to her. Sara gets really angry and says, "He'd better take his hands off of her, or I'll take care of him."

"What cha gonna do?" Clyde asks anxiously.

"I don't know, but I'll think of something."

Just then Ruthie gets a small smile on her face and seems to agree with Jonathan.

"I don't know what that was all about, but I'm going to find out," Sara tells Clyde. To relieve some tension, she picks up a rock and takes her trusty sling shot out of her back pocket. She takes aim at a weather vane on top of the building across the street and lets it go. The next thing they hear is a ping, from the rock ricocheting off the weather vane.

Chapter 17

Ruthie Decides

Mom keeps busy around the house trying to make ends meet. There's not much food to be found and even less work. She wonders how much longer she can come up with the $10 a month for rent; it seems with each month it gets tougher and tougher. Most months it's all the money they can come up with. To survive, they have to barter to put food on the table. Numerous times, the pressure's too much and she sits and weeps. It's so hard to watch her children go without. Like so many others, she doesn't understand what's going on.

Sitting in the front room, Dorris wonders about her family back home and how they're doing. Her mom and dad were upset about her plans to marry Elmer, and when she did, they disowned her. Since leaving home, there's been little to no communication. Still, there are times she thinks about packing up and heading back; she's even gone as far as planning how she'd do it. The family would have to ride the rails, and with no money, there's no hope of doing that. She thinks, *If I was on my own, I'd probably already be gone. At this point, though, there's no turning back.* So here she sits; sewing, mending, and doing any odd job to bring in enough money for the essentials.

Today has been one of those days, which seem to happen more and more frequently, that her emotions get the best of her.

She needs to pull herself together; the kids don't need to see her this way. Wrapping up one of those times, Sara and Clyde come through the front door, walk up to Mom, and give her a hug. They can tell she's been crying, which is tough on them. They love Mom and want to ask her what's wrong, but they know she doesn't want to talk about it.

"Hi, Mom!" Sara and Clyde chime in.

"Hey, you two, would you go get Rachel for me? She's in the other room."

"Sure, Mom, I'll get her," Clyde answers as he leaves the room.

"Sara, how was your day?"

"Oh, it was okay."

"Did you see Ruthie on your way home?"

"Yeah, she was talking with Jonathan," Sara said in disgust.

"Oh? What were they talking about?"

"Don't know; we didn't interrupt."

As they talk, Ruthie comes through the front door. She doesn't seem too excited about being there; in fact, she seems a little distracted.

"Hey!" Mom says as she looks up at Ruthie.

"Oh, hi. I have to change and meet someone. It won't take long."

"Everything okay, Ruthie?"

"Oh yeah, just fine. I got a lead on a job today, and I'm going now to see if I can get it."

"Ruthie!" Mom rejoices. "That's great; we sure can use the money. What are you going to be doing?" Mom asks.

"Not quite sure, but just to work and help out will be great."

"Well, just make sure you know what you're doing. How'd ya hear bout it?"

"Jonathan told me. Got to get going!"

Sara walks into the next room where Clyde is and shares what Ruthie just told Mom. She says, "I don't like this, Clyde. 'Member when Ruthie was shaking her head, as if she was telling him no?"

"Yeah, then he grabbed her."

"Right, then she started agreeing with him."

"Yeah, that's a little strange."

"There's gotta be more to this, but I just can't put it together."

***

Jonathan leaves Ruthie and heads to the WD to talk with Big Al. He walks in as two bouncers stand up next to Al's table. As Jonathan approaches, Al looks up and says, "You'd better have some good news for me!"

"I do. She went home to change and is coming back to talk."

"That's perfect; I can get a look at her myself, up close. She'd better be all you said, no plane Jane."

"Oh, she's a great little filly! I better run. I'll meet her to make sure she comes because she's a little shy."

The owner smirks, "She'll get over that quickly." The two goons let out a big laugh.

Jonathan walks out of the WD and sees Ruthie walking toward him. She's pretty nervous, knowing that if Mom finds out, she'll kill her. She spots Jonathan walking toward her, which calms her down. As he gets closer, he knows why he's attracted to this young lady; she's simply gorgeous. He has a great time just watching her walk. She's wearing a blue patterned dress with pink flowers and a white collar that is buttoned at the neck. The dress hangs mid-calf and shows off her youthful figure. Her light blonde hair and mesmerizing blue eyes are enough to drive any man crazy. She still has that little-girl look, though, with her hair braided in pigtails. Mom made the dress for special occasions; in fact, Ruthie has only two dresses to choose from. Jonathan greets her with a hug and tells her, "You are one cute doll."

Ruthie blushes as Jonathan walks her into the hotel.

He cautions, "Don't be nervous. This is in the bag. The way you look you're going to knock 'em dead."

Going through the big double doors and into the main room, Ruthie slows down and looks around. All the men stop what they're doing and stare. *What are they looking at?* she wonders as her nervousness creeps back.

Jonathan leads her up to the table and introduces her to Big Al by saying, "Mr. Al, this here is Ruthie." Her initial impression is that he makes her uncomfortable. She looks into his eyes and can tell he's scanning her up and down. Every once in a while, he stops and looks into her eyes, which makes her increasingly more uncomfortable.

Jonathan feels the tension and bows out by saying, "I have to go see a man about a dog." Translated, that means he's going to buy some whiskey.

Ruthie, who doesn't understand the translation, turns to Jonathan and says, "I didn't know you were getting a dog." As everyone in the place lets out a loud laugh, her face turns red in embarrassment. She quickly turns back to the owner and says, "What do you want to know?"

He asks, "So Jonathan says you need a job?"

"Yeah, I guess so," she responds sheepishly.

"Well, I have one for you. I'll pay you $4 a week and you work four nights 'til we close. Deal?"

"I don't think I can do that for only $4 a week!" Ruthie protests.

"What? I thought you said you wanted a job!"

"I do, but I can't work until you close. I also have chores to do and school to take care of. Four dollars a week is an insult! If I have to do that, I'll find something else."

"You're a little livewire, aren't you?"

"Don't know what you mean by that, Sir."

"Oh, never mind! Boy, I thought you'd be more grateful, living in my house rent-free and all, but okay, I'll pay you $6 a week and you can stay in the house.

"What do you mean 'rent-free and all'?"

"I don't charge you any rent, haven't since you moved in. Why do you ask?"

"Well, I just thought . . . oh never mind; it doesn't matter anyhow."

"Well now, before we finalize this deal, you need to turn around slowly and let me take a gander at you."

Ruthie turns and all the guys once again stop to have a look. Finally, she says, "Do I have the job?"

"Yeah, I guess you'll do."

"Thanks." She quickly walks out and heads home, really confused. She thought Mom told her she was paying $10 rent. In fact, she remembers seeing Mom give Jonathan the rent money. Ruthie scans the street for Jonathan, but he's nowhere to be found. She thinks, *I have to get to the bottom of this.* She second guesses herself, not too sure if she can follow through, and besides, what's she going to tell Mom?

***

Its dusk and Clyde and Sara are out doing the last chores of the day. These are always the hardest; working or going to school, then having to work until the sun goes down is tiring and Sara complains, "Why does Ruthie always seem to have something else to do? She's never around when we need her help!"

"Yeah, she always slips away, and Mom lets her get away with it. Where'd she go tonight?" Clyde asks, siding with Sara.

"I don't know. She didn't say where, just that she had an interview for a job."

"A real job?" questions Clyde.

"Yeah, I guess so. Don't know what she can do, though."

Just as Sara finishes, Ruthie walks up and answers, "I heard what you said, and by the way, I did get the job."

"Oh, hip, hip, hooray! What cha doing, sweeping the store?"

"No, I'm, aaah, I'm, oh never mind! It doesn't matter to you, anyway."

"Yeah, I know. Ya say that all the time, 'You're too little to understand'," Sara retorts.

"That's right! Where's Mom?"

"In the house, I guess."

Too Old, Too Fast

Ruthie walks toward the house thinking, *What should I tell Mom? It has to be doing something for someone she doesn't know. Boy, that'll be tough because Mom knows about everyone. It has to be something that I can be out late at night for a few nights a week. Oh, I don't know what to say! Wait a minute; a new family just took over the ranch Jonathan's working at. They have a little boy. I'll tell Mom I'm going to be a nanny to the Goldberg's little boy. That's it, they hardly ever come into town, and they keep to themselves. In the three months they've been here, they've only been in town a couple of times. They live on the outskirts, so it won't take long to even walk there. Perfect plan!*

As she walks into the house, Mom greets her with a hug and kiss on the cheek. Sitting down at the table together, Mom asks, "Well, did you get the job?"

"Yes, I did!"

"That's wonderful; tell me about it."

"Well, the only thing I know is, I'll be taking care of a little boy."

"How old?"

"Not sure."

"What days?"

"Not sure, but I don't think they'll always be the same. It's going to be three or four evenings a week."

"That's quite a bit, don't you think? How much are they paying you?"

"Oh, I can handle it! They're paying $4 dollars a week."

"That's pretty good pay for so few hours."

"That's what I thought, too. They must have a lot of money."

"Well, that'll surely help around here," Dorris concludes.

★★★

Jonathan walks back into the hotel with a big smile on his face.

"Well, what ya think, big guy?" Jonathan inquires sarcastically.

154

"We'll see, we'll see," Big Al responds. "You know, that little girl sure seems confused."

"What cha mean?" Jonathan asks with a puzzled look.

"Ya know, Whiskey, when we talked about pay, she got a little upset."

"Really, I wonder why she'd do that," Jonathan replies.

"Don't quite understand it myself," Big Al responds. "Her mom must not let her know very much."

"Why ya say that?" Jonathan questions.

"'Cause when I told her that they could continue to live in that house for free, she seemed a little confused."

Jonathan tries to show no expression, but his insides are jumping like a frog from a lily pad. "What'd she say? Was she grateful?"

"Not quite sure, but she took the job."

"Well, that's good; I need to get back to the ranch to get things ready for tomorrow. See ya'll later." Jonathan turns on his heels and walks out of the room, thinking, *Oh, boy, what am I going to do now? Ruthie knows what's been happening. I hope the big guy doesn't suspect anything. If he finds out what I've been doing, I'll be in big trouble.*

Big Al looks at the bouncers and says, "Keep an eye on him. I don't trust him; he's up to something."

Chapter 18

Payback Time

Ruthie's been working for a few weeks and with the extra income they've been able to make ends meet. While not to the point of plenty, they're far better off than they have been. Mom's so happy with Ruthie's job that she no longer questions her each night.

It pleases Ruthie to see Mom smiling more. Even though she doesn't care for the environment she has to work in, she thinks, *I have to do all I can to help out the family.* That's the only thing that keeps her going back. She wants to talk to Jonathan, but hasn't seen him since she started to work. One day a couple of ranch hands she's seen with Jonathan sit down at a table. She walks up to them and asks, "Either of you seen Jonathan?" One states, "Oh yeah, he's out rounding up cattle." Hearing that comes as a surprise; Jonathan's never talked about doing that before, but she figures, *Now days you have to do all you can to make a living, whether you like it or not. I know all about that.*

***

Jonathan heads back to the ranch, knowing he's in trouble with Ruthie. When he arrives, the Goldbergs ask him to gather a couple of men to round-up cattle. Wanting to disappear for a few days, he sees this as an opportunity and quickly volunteers.

He thinks, *If I leave town for a while, things may just blow over.* He knows that rarely works, but it's worth a try and a viable reason to head toward the mountains for the time being. *You know, never do today what you can put off until tomorrow or something like that,* he thinks.

A group of six head out and for the first couple of days, Jonathan really enjoys the open plains. Along about the third day, he gets a feeling that someone's watching, but he can't quite put it together. Right around dusk, he asks one of the riders, "I've got this funny feeling we're being watched. What about you?"

"Oh yeah, ya haven't noticed?"

"Noticed what?"

"There's been a couple of guys tailing us since we left, but I saw them ride back toward town today. Not sure what they were lookin' for, though."

"Ya ever seen 'em before?"

"Yeah, a couple of times in town. In the WD, seems like."

Jonathan can't quite figure it out, but tells his partner, "Let me know if ya see 'em again."

"Sure enough."

***

Clyde finds work wherever he can, and every spare moment is spent at the Livingstons' with Warrior. They've become close and Warrior's his best friend. He thinks, *When Dad was alive, I didn't understand why he trusted Sacred so much, how he could spend so much time with him, but now I do.* Clyde and Harold have taken their time breaking Warrior, but today's the day for the real test when Clyde gets on his back and rides him, hopefully.

As they walk to the corral, Harold can tell Clyde's nervous; he talks nonstop and asks the same questions over and over. They've taken this past week to prepare Warrior for this ride by placing a saddle on him, then walking him around in the corral. Today will be different. Though it'll start the same, the second time around Harold will lead Warrior to the fence where Clyde will climb on. Harold holds the halter and leads Warrior, while Clyde walks alongside and holds the reigns as he talks to Warrior the entire lap. Harold inches Warrior closer to the fence as Clyde climbs it with reins in hand. Warrior nervously tries to pull back, but Harold holds his ground and puts pressure on the halter while Clyde swings his leg over Warrior's back. Clyde settles in on the leather saddle as Harold leads Warrior around the corral, amazed that he's not putting up much of a fight.

Clyde thinks *This is great! I've waited so long to be on the back of my horse. Boy, if Dad could only see me now*! As he relaxes, Warrior decides enough is enough. He jerks his head back, snaps the halter from Harold's hand, and moves on his own. Harold hollers, "Hang on, Clyde, you're going for a ride! Pull back on the reigns to let him know who's in charge."

Clyde thinks, *If this is being in charge, I'm in trouble*!

Warrior starts out with a couple of short little hops and then bucks as Clyde hangs on for dear life. He then takes a short sprint, stops, raises his hind quarters off the ground and gives Clyde air space between his rump and the saddle. Holding on with all he has and squeezing Warrior's ribs with his legs, it feels like he's been riding all day. Trying all he can to bring this to a close, Clyde talks to Warrior in between bucks. He must recognize Clyde's voice, because he soon settles down and calmly walks around with Clyde securely on his back.

***

Mom, Sara and Ruthie are sitting around the house talking about their day when Ruthie looks at the clock and realizes she's going to be late for work. Clyde runs in as Ruthie sprints out, almost running him over. "Sorry, Clyde. Hope I didn't scare you. Got to go!" Ruthie hurriedly says as she heads to work.

"Hey Ruthie, I rode Warrior today!"

"Yeah, that's nice. See you later," she responds, as Clyde looks discouraged.

Sara grabs him by the arm and says, "Come on, let's get the chores done!"

"We don't need to hurry! I just got home! Besides, did ya hear me? I rode Warrior!"

"Clyde, be quiet, let's go," Sara demands.

"Sara, I want to tell Mom."

"Not now, we have to go."

"Go? Go where? What about our chores?" Clyde asks.

Gritting her teeth, she responds in a low growl to where Mom can't hear, "Forget the chores and be quiet. We're going to follow Ruthie. Something's not right."

"What cha mean?"

"Things don't fit! Ruthie gets this job, doesn't talk much about it, smells different when she comes home and besides that, I found extra money in her jewelry box. Just follow me!"

Clyde eagerly whispers, "Okay, this is going to be fun! Don't get too close, and make sure we stay in the shadows."

Sara shakes her head, "Just hurry!"

Ruthie hurries to the WD. As she gets close, she spots Jonathan riding in a car. As it slows, Jonathan jumps out and runs up to Ruthie. "Hey, how's my little filly?" Jonathan hollers, running up with his arms open wide.

"I don't have time for you now; I'm late!" snaps Ruthie.

"What? No time for the man of your dreams?"

With a disgusted glance, Ruthie shakes her head and keeps running.

Clyde and Sara, not too far behind, stand across the street in the shadows to observe.

Sara whispers to Clyde, "That's it, Ruthie, let him have it! Don't listen to him; go on to work."

"Yeah!" Clyde chimes in. "Look, Ruthie's going into the WD. I wonder why she's stopping there. She's goin' ta be late for work."

This don't seem right, Sara ponders. "Let's hang out and see what happens."

"Boy, this sure is fun!" Clyde says, rubbing his hands together.

Jonathan follows Ruthie into the hotel and heads toward the back. Every night Ruthie works, she leaves home with normal clothes on and changes into her dress for the evening in the backroom. She has a large assortment of outfits to choose from, and tonight she chooses a tightly fitting dress that shows her girly figure. Jonathan waits for her just outside the door as she changes. She opens the door, sees Jonathan standing there and says, "I have to get going! I can't talk now."

"Just tell me! Ya mad at me?"

"You could say that!"

"Yeah, I know. I'm sorry for not telling ya I had to leave for a couple weeks."

"That has nothing to do with it, and like I said, I don't have time."

As she squeezes through the doorway to get by him, Jonathan says, "Hold up there for a minute." He touches her neck and pulls the shoulder straps down to just below the shoulders. "You need to show a little skin."

Ruthie looks right through him and threatens, "Don't you ever touch me like that again!" She's having one of those days when nothing seems to go right. Jonathan follows her into the bar.

Clyde and Sara are bewildered about what's going on and wonder why Ruthie's still in the hotel. Clyde gets impatient, looks at Sara, and says, "I'm going in to check it out. We've been waiting here for over an hour."

In disgust, Sara responds, "Clyde, it hasn't been an hour. Boy, are you impatient."

Clyde says, "If she don't hurry, she'll get fired. She's so late."

Sara ducks behind a motor vehicle, pulls Clyde down by her, and says, "Look! Here comes Jonathan! But where's Ruthie?"

Jonathan walks out of the bar to get some fresh air and stands in front of the big double doors. Inside, Ruthie's serving tables. There's a guy sitting at one of her tables who's given her a bad time since she started. As she walks by, he leans back in his chair, slaps her on the butt, and laughs. This pushes her over the edge. Overwhelmed with emotion, she cries and then gets so mad that she allowed him to reduce her to tears. As she turns to walk out, she gives the leg of his chair a big kick and over he goes. She heads out the double doors with her head in her hands, crying uncontrollably.

By this time, Clyde and Sara have worked their way through the darkness to the hotel and are able to see some of what's going on inside. They can see really well through a side window, but it's pretty difficult to hear.

Sara says, "Let's stay here for a couple minutes and see what happens!"

"Look! Who's that coming out the door crying?" Clyde points out.

"That looks like Ruthie, but she doesn't own a dress like that. That is Ruthie! What's she doing in that trampy looking dress?"

"Shh! Listen, Jonathan's talking to her."

"I'm done! I'm not doing this any more," sobs Ruthie.

"Now, now, take a minute and think about it. You're helping the family and getting a discount on your rent."

"Yeah, that's what I want to talk to you about!"

"What? Talk about what?"

"The rent!" Ruthie hollers, her anger taking rein over her tears.

"What about the rent?" Jonathan questions. He knows he's had it, and needs to come up with something fast. Being gone those two weeks, he's thought of all sorts of stories, but which one does he use?

"You told us Big Al's charging us $10 a month for rent, and during my interview, he told me we're living there rent-free. What have ya done with the money?"

"Ruthie, Ruthie, do you think I'd take advantage of the family for my own personal gain? That really hurts; I thought you knew me better than that."

"Well, I thought I did too, but the facts are the facts." Ruthie says without hesitation.

"Listen up, my little filly. I was saving this as a surprise for you and your mom, but since this has come out, I'll tell you the truth." That's something Jonathan rarely does, but he continues, "The money you've paid me, I've taken an' saved it. I'm working with someone else to get you a place of your own."

"Are you serious? Jonathan, I can't believe it! What a wonderful thing you're doing!" With that, Ruthie gives him a hug and a peck on the cheek.

Clyde and Sara aren't the only ones listening to the conversation. The two big bouncers Al told to follow Jonathan are just inside the door. They look at each other and head to the back of the bar. Sara looks at Clyde and says, "He's lying through his big pearly white teeth. Clyde, I swear I'm going to get him one of these days."

Jonathan assures Ruthie, "Now, my little filly, you need to go back in there and finish up."

"Jonathan, I told you. I'm done, no more."

Jonathan grabs her by the shoulders and threatens, "You get your fancy little butt back in there right now, or I'll make things pretty miserable for ya. And that money your Mom paid me, you guys will never see it."

Ruthie can't believe her ears! After what Jonathan just said, now he threatens her!

Sara and Clyde never did believe Jonathan's story. Sara, about to bust a button, looks at Clyde and says, "I'm going back a few motor vehicles, and then I'll cross the street where they can't see me and hide right over there." She points directly across from the hotel. There are numerous buggies parked on the street and she can hide behind one that's in the alley. She continues, "You wait right here. I'll be right back."

Clyde grabs her arm and says, "Don't do anything dumb."

"I won't," she quickly responds.

Ruthie, once again, begins to cry. With his hands on her shoulders, Jonathan spins her around and pushes her toward the big double doors. He swings them open, slaps her on the butt and says, "Back to work!"

Sara witnesses everything and she's had enough of Jonathan. She searches the ground for a rock for her sling shot, thinking, *the bigger, the better*. Jonathan walks off the sidewalk with a big toothy grin on his face, chuckling. He says to himself, "Boy, did I handle that one! I have her right where I want her."

When Ruthie walks back in, big Al's sitting at the corner table thinking, *That little gal has a lot of spunk.* The bouncers walk up, sit down, and share with Al what they heard Jonathan tell Ruthie. About that time, the cowboy that Ruthie put in his place walks up and grabs her arm. Al motions to the bouncers to take care of this guy. They walk up behind him, grab him by his Wranglers, and head to the double doors. With one mighty toss, the cowboy sails over the hood of a motor vehicle and lands in the dirt road, just missing Jonathan. He turns to look at the commotion and laughs as he points at the guy who's face-down in the dirt.

Sara finds a perfect rock for her sling shot and thinks, *This is the biggest one I've ever tried to shoot. Hope it doesn't ruin my aim,* as she focuses in on her target. Clyde watches from across the street and tries to get her attention by waving his arms and jumping up and down, but it's no use. He knows what she's about to do and it's not going to be good. He has to stop her, so he moves up the street, darts between a couple of buggies, and sprints toward Sara, but it's too late.

Ruthie looks at Al and mouths, "Thank you." The bouncers walk back in and up to Al's table where he looks at them and says, "I want to talk with Jonathan. Now!"

Sara takes aim, thinking, *I'll go for his crotch.* She leans against the buggie to steady the sling shot and, in a split second, lets it go. Jonathan's laughing so hard he doubles over as Sara releases the rock, which sails straight as an arrow, right on track, hitting the target square. There's just one problem; the target moved, and instead of hitting him in his privates, it hits him right in his big toothy grin with such force that it knocks him off balance and onto his back. He realizes his perfect teeth are no longer perfect as he lies there on his back holding a tooth in his one hand and spitting another to the ground. He has no idea what just happened, but blood flows freely with every spit.

Clyde can't believe she really did it. Now they're in big trouble, and Sara's frozen in her tracks. He grabs her, but she doesn't budge. "Come on, Sara, we've got to get out of here, *now*!" It doesn't do any good. Clyde thinks maybe this is what Dad meant when he would say someone was "scared stiff." The bouncers walk out the hotel doors and see Jonathan lying there spitting out blood.

About that time, the sheriff walks up and asks, "What's going on?"

One bouncer replies, "Don't know, Sheriff. I just walked out and saw him lying there."

A vehicle stops in the road and the passenger says, "Hey, Sheriff, I think that one guy lying over there kicked him and put 'im down."

Looking around, the sheriff notices two figures in the shadows behind a car across the street. They're not very big; in fact, they look like kids. Clyde grabs Sara and again tries to get her to move.

The sheriff tells the bouncers, "I'm going over to those two across the street to find out if they saw anything."

"Okay, Sheriff, we'll take care of Jonathan," they replied with a smile.

Chapter 19

Everybody Runs

Clyde peeks over the hood and notices the sheriff walking toward them. "Come on, Sara, we gotta get outta here; the sheriff's coming!" With that, Sara comes to her senses, grabs Clyde's arm, and they run off with the sheriff close behind.

He picks up his pace and hollers, "You two, stop right there!" They head home as fast as they can with Sara hot on Clyde's heals when she cries, "Clyde, I dropped my slingshot!"

"Just keep running! He'll never catch us," Clyde responds.

Huffing and puffing, Sara asks, "Clyde, did I kill 'im?"

"Don't know; stop talkin' and run."

The sheriff has them in sight, but is in no hurry to chase them, figuring they're running home anyway. As they slow down to a stop in front of their house, he says to himself, "Just who I thought it was. I think I'll go back and ask Jonathan some questions before I confront Dorris and the kids." Retracing his steps, he notices the sling-shot on the ground and picks it up as evidence.

The bouncers take Jonathan inside the hotel, up the stairs, and into his room. He's bleeding pretty good, so the bouncers grab some towels and tell him to hold them over his mouth. He settles down in a chair just as the door opens and Big Al walks in.

"What happened to you?"

Barely able to talk, with slurred words, he replies, "Not too sure. Something hit me in the mouth; felt like a boulder."

"That's okay, 'cause you don't need to talk much. Just listen and answer my questions. Tell me about that family living in my home; you know, Ruthie's family."

He mumbles, "What ya want to know?"

"They're there rent-free, right?" Al asks with a look of concern.

To delay having to answer and to give himself some time to think, Jonathan readjusts the towels he's holding to his mouth. He weighs the consequences of his answer. "Sure, that's what you said before they moved in, right? You know, six months?"

"You sure about that?" Al questions.

"Yeah, that's what ya told me."

Turning to the bouncers, Al says, "Boys, tell him what you overheard."

They retell the conversation between Jonathan and Ruthie. As he sits there, Jonathan knows he's in deep trouble. They don't quite finish their story before Al interrupts them, visibly upset. Jonathan knows he'll pay for stealing from him; it's just a matter of how much pain and how far they'll go. The bouncers are big, strong guys, and Jonathan tries to think how he'll respond if given the opportunity. Al looks at the bouncers and nods his head. As they move toward Jonathan, someone knocks on the door, stopping them in their tracks. Al reaches over and opens it.

The sheriff says, "I need to speak with Jonathan."

Al replies, "Sure Sheriff, come on in." Jonathan gives a sigh of relief. With his eyes securely on Al, he mumbles through the towels, "Good to see ya, Sheriff."

The sheriff ambles over and says, "Hope I'm not interrupting anything, but I have a question for you. I think I know what happened. Do you want to press charges?"

"Not sure, Sheriff. I still don't know what happened."

"Well, it looks like two kids playing around with their slingshot hit you with a rock."

"How'd they do that?"

"The best I figure is they were playing around with this."
He pulls the sling out of his back pocket. "When I got there, I
saw 'em across the street. Once I headed in their direction, they
took off and must have dropped the sling shot on the ground. I
couldn't catch 'em, you know how fast you can run when you're
scared, but I followed 'em home. Once I saw who it was, I
decided to come back and ask if you wanted to press charges."

Jonathan, curious to know who did it, asks, "Who was it?"

"It was Dorris' two kids; you know, the girl and boy."

"Clyde and Sara?" Jonathan asks, surprised.

Grinning, Al asks, "You mean Ruthie's kid sister and
brother?" .

"Yeah, those are the two."

It doesn't take Jonathan long to reply, "Nah, I won't press
charges. But Sheriff, scare 'em to death and teach 'em a lesson.
You know, tell 'em something really bad is going to happen to
'em."

"Sure, I can do that, but are you sure you don't want to press
charges?"

"Yep," Jonathan grimaces through the pain. He thinks, *If
I press charges, I'll need to stay in town. I need to get out of
town! Besides, I have bigger problems to deal with.*

The sheriff says, "I better head to the house; got some
unfinished work to do."

"See ya later, Sheriff." Al responds.

As he turns to leave, the sheriff asks Jonathan, "You going
to be okay? You need to get that mouth looked at."

"Thanks, Sheriff, I'll make sure to do that. See ya later."

The sheriff looks at Al and says, "Could you send one of
your guys and get Doc for him? And can I talk with you for a
minute?"

"Sure!" Al replies. He glances over at the bouncers and
sends one to get the doc and the other for ice and a spittoon.
As they leave, Jonathan sees this as an opportunity to escape
through the open window, so he grabs a few things and makes
his way toward it. He can hear the sheriff and Al talking and

knows the goons will be back soon. If he's going to get away, now's the time to do it.

Ruthie hears the commotion, but continues to work; unaware of what's going on.

Clyde and Sara run to the house. When they look back, they don't see the sheriff. Clyde says, "We lost 'im! Boy, I thought we were dead."

Sara repeats, "Clyde, did I kill 'im?"

"Nah, I don't think so, but why'd ya do it?"

Slowing down to take a few deep breaths, Sara answers, "You know, I was so mad at the way he treated Ruthie, I just let it fly."

"I know! I tried to get your attention, but you were pretty focused. Ya didn't even see me."

Not wanting to arouse Mom's suspicion, they stop just outside, wipe off the sweat, and take a couple of deep breaths. Clyde asks, "What are we tellin' Mom?"

"Nothing about anything, you hear?"

"Nothing?" Clyde asks.

"Nothing! Swear you won't say anything!"

"Okay, okay, I won't say nothin'." Clyde responds hesitantly.

"Now, ya swear, Clyde. If you say anything, I'll never talk to you again, you hear?"

"Yeah, yeah, I hear ya." Raising his right hand he says, "I swear."

When they open the door and walk in, Mom asks, "Where you been? You've been gone a while."

"Just finishin' up the chores. Then we went for a walk," Sara answers.

"That's right; went for a walk, a long walk," Clyde repeats.

Sara glares at him, as if to say "Be quiet."

***

Jonathan slides out the window and onto the roof. He spots Doc below on the street with one of the big guys. Then he heads toward the hotel, and hears the other stomping up the stairs. He edges along the roof, over the backside, and finds a drainpipe to slide down. Once down, he knows he needs to head out of town and thinks, *I need cash. I'll head over to the Goldberg's to collect my pay and get out of town.* He then disappears into the cover of night.

The doctor, bouncers, and Al enter the room and look around. Jonathan's nowhere to be found. Doc asks, "Where'd he go?"

Al moves to the window and stares out, gritting his teeth. "Guess he had somewhere else to be!"

The sheriff heads over to the Lewis's, pondering how he'll tell Dorris what's happened, as well as how he's going to put a scare into her two children. As he approaches the house, he notices they have just a few lights on and thinks, *They must be getting ready for bed. Doesn't matter, I have to take care of business*, as he raps on the front door.

Clyde and Sara hurry into their room. Sara grabs Clyde by the back of the shirt and says, "You almost blew it! Watch what you say."

"Yeah, yeah, I know. It's just tough lying to Mom. If she ever finds out, she'll skin us alive."

"If ya don't say anything, ya ain't lying—and besides, she'll never know."

About that time there comes a knock on the front door. Sara looks at Clyde in bewilderment and asks, "Who can that be?"

"Probably Jonathan looking fer ya," he says, taunting her.

"Nah, nobody saw us," Sara declares, and then wrinkles her nose, "I don't think!"

Dorris answers the door with a surprised look on her face, "Evening, Sheriff. What brings you here?"

"Evening, Dorris. May I come in?"

"Sure!"

As Mom answers the front door, Clyde slowly cracks the bedroom door. Clyde turns to Sara and warns, "You're in big trouble! The sheriff's afta ya."

"Ha, ha, that's not funny. You sure can be mean at times and now's not the right time."

"Sara, I'm not being funny! The sheriff's here! Look!"

Sara peeks out and gasps, "Oh boy, I've got to run and hide. Help me, Clyde!"

The sheriff steps inside and states, "Dorris, we had a situation down by the hotel tonight, and I was wondering if the kids have been home all evening?"

"Yeah, they've been out doing their chores and just came in a few minutes ago."

"Mind if I talk to them?"

"No, not at all. I'll get them."

"Thanks, Dorris."

Sara scampers around the room and gathers up some clothes to take with her as Clyde quietly opens the window for their escape. With her arms full, Sara has one leg out the window as Dorris opens the bedroom door. She's really confused until she peers into the room and sees Sara climbing out the window. "Where do you think you're going, little girl?"

"Nowhere, Mom."

"Then what are you doing climbing out the window?"

"I dropped something and I'm climbing out to get it."

"Carrying clothes?" Mom asks.

Clyde stands there shaking his head, knowing they're cooked. He rolls his eyes and thinks, *Sara, keep quiet! You're just digging us deeper.*

Mom's face turns bright red. "I want you two out in the front room—pronto!"

"But, Mom!"

"Now!"

Both dart into the front room where the sheriff's waiting, and greet their visitor, "Evening, Sheriff."

"Evening, you two. I've got a couple of questions for you."

Mom inserts, "And you better tell him the truth or you won't sit down for a week. Got it?"

In unison they reply, "Yes Ma'am."

The sheriff asks, "Where have you been over the last hour?"

Looking at Mom, Sara answers, "Well, sir, we . . . were out doing our chores. Ain't that right, Clyde?"

"Yeah, I guess," Clyde says with hesitation.

"What do you mean 'you guess'?" the sheriff questions.

Sara glances at Clyde, which prompts him to respond, "Hey, we were out doing chores!"

"Were you two down by the hotel this evening?" the sheriff questions.

"Well, we may have taken a short break from our chores to take a walk . . . right Clyde?"

"Yeah, a real short break, not long enough to get into trouble or nothin'."

Sara looks down, shakes her head and whispers, "Clyde, please be quiet."

The sheriff pulls Sara's slingshot out of his back pocket and taps it in his hand. Then he looks at Sara and admits, "Sara, I saw you standing there and followed you back home here. Why don't you tell me what happened?"

Sara cracks and cries, "I'm sorry, Mom, but I didn't like the way he was treating Ruthie. Did I kill 'im?"

"Ruthie!" Mom yells. "What does she have to do with a killing?"

The sheriff jumps in, "Everyone calm down, Sara didn't kill anyone. The kids simply created a situation downtown that caused a ruckus."

Sara continues, "Mom, we followed Ruthie to work, just to see what's going on. Jonathan got mad at her, grabbed her, an' hurt her. Then, when she went back into the hotel, he laughed about it. So I got mad and picked up a rock. I was aiming for his privates, but he bent over and it hit him in the face."

Dorris covers her face to hide a half-grin and responds, "Oh, Lordy! Sara, how could you do such a thing?"

Knowing they're in trouble, Clyde starts to cry as Sara explains, "Mom, I just wanted him to keep his hands off Ruthie."

"You keep saying *Ruthie*. Ruthie's at work at the Goldberg's."

"No, Mom, Ruthie's working at the hotel."

"Yeah, Dorris, I thought you knew that," the sheriff replies. "Actually, she works in the bar."

"What? You mean my daughter's working in that kind of place with those types of women for a guy like Big Al?" Mom looks for her coat, and then turns to the sheriff and says, "Do what you have to with these two. I'm going to get my daughter."

Dorris makes a beeline for the WD, and by the time she gets there, she's pretty worked up. She goes over in her mind, *How can Ruthie do this? What would drive her to do such a thing?* Talking to herself stirs up her emotions so high that when she walks in, she's like a momma bear looking for her cub; no one had better get in her way. She flings open the double doors and makes a hard left into the bar. As she storms in, she catches the attention of everyone. Glancing around and not seeing Ruthie amongst the women, she hollers, "Ruthie!"

★★★

Shocked at how fast Dorris left, the sheriff wonders what to do with the kids. He looks at Clyde and Sara and orders, "You two . . . grab your little sister and come with me. Now!"

"Are we under arrest?"

"I don't know right now, but you're going to my office."

As they all leave, it dawns on him that Dorris may be headed for trouble, so he'd better get over there just in case. As he picks up his pace, the kids can barely keep up. Approaching the bar, he turns to the kids and says, "You all head over to my office and take a seat. Don't either one of you move from there, or I'll lock you up and throw away the key."

By this time Clyde and Sara are pretty scared and question just what's going to happen to them. They pick up Rachel and answer, "Yes sir." Running to the office, they scurry inside and close the door.

Dorris again hollers, "Ruthie!"

Seeing her coming through the door, Ruthie hides in a corner where she can't be seen. Since it's clearly not going to take long for Mom to find her; she decides to step out. "Here I am, Mom." Ruthie's face is bright red from embarrassment and tears stream down her cheeks.

Dorris turns on her heel, and looking in Ruthie's direction, breaks into a deep sob. With a broken voice, she walks over and asks, "Ruthie, what are you doing in a place like this?"

Big Al and the bouncers hear the commotion and come into the bar. Al tells Ruthie to get back to work and turns to talk to Dorris.

She walks up to Al and, nose to nose, tells him, "My daughter will not work here any longer! Do you understand?"

The bouncers walk up behind and reach to grab her when the sheriff walks through the doors and hollers, "I wouldn't touch her if I were you!"

Al protests, "Hey, I worked a deal for you! You live in my home rent-free, and one of the conditions is that your daughter works for me. So, I own her right now."

The sheriff walks up as Dorris fumes, "You listen to me, Mr. Big Shot. Nobody owns my daughter. I've paid rent since we moved in! She's not going to work here or for you anymore. Got that?" Mom turns to Ruthie, points to the door and says, "You go change right now. You're coming home with me."

Al again protests and the sheriff steps in, "Let's all give it a rest tonight; everyone's upset. Go home, sleep on it, and we'll see what we can come up with later."

As Dorris and Ruthie enter the lobby, Ruthie says, "Mom, I still need to change."

Mom replies, "Go get your clothes, we're getting out of this place."

Ruthie walks into the back room, grabs her clothes, meets Mom, and they head home. As they walk, Mom starts to fill Ruthie in on what's developed. The sheriff walks out of the WD and hollers for them to stop. He runs up to them, explains that the kids are in his office, and shares his plan to put a scare into them.

When they walk into the office, Clyde and Sara are sitting by the desk with scared looks, and Rachel is sitting in the sheriff's chair by the window. Mom picks Rachel up, walks to the other side of the room, and sits in one of the wooden chairs. Ruthie, still embarrassed over tonight's goings on, stands off by herself clutching her clothes in an attempt to hide the floozy dress she has on. The sheriff walks over to his desk, sits on the edge, and says, "I want you two to understand the trouble you're in."

"Yes, sir."

"I'm going to have to lock you up."

"What? We're going to jail? But we're just kids!" Clyde protests.

"I know, but there's not much more I can do. You broke the law, and we have to punish criminals."

"Mom, please help!" Clyde pleads.

"Not much I can do; you're in the hands of the law now."

"But I didn't do it! Sara did."

"Thanks, Clyde."

"But it's true!"

"Well, you were there, Clyde, and that's just like doing it," the sheriff replies.

Clyde cries and begs not to go to jail. Sara's scared, too, but she holds her composure. She's not going to let anyone see how scared she is.

"Come with me." The children follow the sheriff as he leads them to the back room, opens the cell door, and directs them in. He slams the door to make an impact, a sound he hopes they will never want to hear again. Then he turns, walks back to the front office and says to the kids, "I'll have to check out your story. It may take a while, so make yourself comfortable." He gives Dorris a wink and whispers, "We'll let them sit there for a while to think about it."

Chapter 20

You Have to Leave

While the sheriff, Mom, and Ruthie are out in the front office, Clyde and Sara sit in a cell in the back. It seems like forever to these two, but in reality it's been less than an hour. They're scared and they keep going over in their minds all that happened. Sara's sitting with her back to Clyde when he asks, "Ya mad at me?"

"What do ya think? I thought we weren't going to say nothin'!"

"I wasn't, but he kind of tricked me," Clyde explained.

"No, he didn't! I was right there, remember?" Sara replies.

Sara, he already knew! He had your slingshot. Just drop it!"

"No, I won't! You brought it up! Clyde, ya didn't back me up, and I don't think I'll ever forgive ya for that."

"If that's the way ya want it, that's fine with me. I just don't want to talk about it."

"Fine!" Sara snaps.

"Double-fine," Clyde retorts, trying to "one up" his sister while turning his back to her. Just as Clyde finishes, the sheriff opens the door and steps over to the cell with a smile on his face.

"Well, you've been cleared. The evidence shows it was a matter of defending your sister." He takes the key down from the wall and opens the door. "You're free to go, but I have some friendly advice for you. Don't do anything like that again; next time, the outcome may be different. If you see something like that happening, let the law handle it for you."

Clyde looks at Sara and replies in a relieved tone, "Oh, we won't . . . will we, Sara?"

Sara nods, still really mad at Clyde. The sheriff steps out of the way while the kids step out of the cell. Sara thinks, *One down, and one to go. This one's probably the easiest, Mom won't be so understanding. Now the real explaining begins.* They walk into the outer office where Mom and Ruthie wait and where Rachel sleeps in Mom's lap. Seeing Ruthie, they run over to give her hugs. She looks at Sara and scolds, "Mom told me what you did. You shouldn't have done that."

Sara counters, "I know, but he was treating you so mean. Is he all right? Where is he?"

"He's okay, I guess. Someone said he lost a couple of teeth. They saw him heading out of town, probably trying to find a dentist."

Mom looks at them and orders, "You two, get home right now. We'll be right behind."

★★★

Jonathan heads out of town as fast as he can. He needs traveling money so his first stop will be the Goldberg's, who owe him a week's pay. Knowing the bouncers will come looking for him, he'll head east. If they find him, it won't be pretty. Jonathan thinks, *I can't believe they're coming after me for $60. How stupid that they'd waste their time.*

With no lights on in the house as he pulls in the Goldberg's driveway, he thinks, *They're either asleep or not at home.* He knocks on the front door. When no one answers, he thinks, *They must be gone.* Grabbing the door knob, he gives it a gentle twist; it's unlocked! "Oh, that's right, they always leave it unlocked," he remembers as he walks in. He knows the right thing would be to wait for their return, but he has no time to waste, so he heads straight to the parlor and rummages through the drawers.

Finally, in the back of the top desk drawer, he finds a stack of cash. He knew it had to be there somewhere, since there's no bank in town, and everyone keeps their cash at home. What surprises him, though, is that this is a pretty obvious place. He ponders, *It can't always be this easy, can it? Oh well, got to get a move on.* He doesn't want to take it all, but it's tempting. Still with enough conscience left to know the Goldberg's need to feed their family, he takes what he's owed, plus a little more for traveling money, closes the drawer, and heads out. Almost to the door, he hears footsteps and voices on the porch, so he turns around and runs back through the kitchen to the back door. Just as he slips out, Mrs. Goldberg and her son come through the front door. Out in the backyard he notices the supply shed to his right and deliberates, *Do I need any supplies?* Deciding to take a look, he steps into the shed and contemplates what he may need. Glancing around, he decides to grab a couple of small boxes of TNT with fuses. As he exits the shed and turns the corner, he almost runs into Mr. Goldberg.

"Jonathan, what are ya doing?"

As Jonathan begins to answer, he hears a car quickly approaching and knows who it likely is. "Can't explain now; I have to go. I'm sorry, Mr. Goldberg, but I quit, and I found some money for my final pay. Have a great life!" Mr. Goldberg stands there, stunned, not knowing what to do or say as Jonathan takes off on a dead run to his car.

***

The bouncers look around town for Jonathan and find out that he was last seen heading east in his 1929 Nash Cabriolet he won in a Poker game just last year. They know he needs to grab some money and is probably headed to the Goldberg's, so off they go, hoping to catch him before he gets too far away.

***

Jonathan throws his stash in the back of the car and speeds off down the dirt road, headed to who knows where. All he knows is that he can no longer stay around here. As he drives away, his mind wanders to his Ruthie. *What a great girl! I'm going to miss her, but there's plenty more fish in the sea.* As he drives away with the moonlight in his side mirror, he glances at his reflection. His upper lip is split open, he's lost his pretty smile, and he's a fugitive—all within the past few hours. Not only have his looks changed, but so has his life. The decisions he's made over these past few months have put him right where he is. With each passing thought and each glance into the mirror, his thoughts turn to revenge. *One day I'll get even, I'll pay them all back.*

***

A week or so passes with Clyde and Sara still in Mom's "dog house." She told them, "You two should have come to me instead of taking matters into your own hands."

They both told Mom they were sorry, but they haven't spoken to each other except when they have to. Ruthie apologized to Mom and told her the whole story about Jonathan. After hearing about all that he did, Mom's pretty upset. The way she put it is, "I'd like to wring his neck!" Mom always says stuff like that when she's upset, but she really doesn't mean it. Anyway, on this day she's supposed to meet the sheriff at the hotel with Big Al to negotiate the rent. As she prepares for the meeting, she instructs the kids to get their work done while she's gone.

It's the first time she's been back since taking Ruthie home. When she walks through the double doors, Al's standing there to greet her and says, "Afternoon, Dorris, you look chipper today!"

"Thank you. Can we get down to business, please?"

"Sure," he tersely responds.

The sheriff walks in as they sit down at a round table in the corner. Dorris and Al greet him as he walks up and invite him to pull up a chair.

Big Al begins, "Since Ruthie left, my business has dropped off. I'd love to have her back. In fact, I'll pay her $10 a week and leave your rent where it is."

"Ruthie is not coming back here . . . not in a million years . . . not for a million dollars."

"Okay, if that's the way you want it, I need $20 a month rent for the house!"

"What? You know I can't afford that! I don't even have a steady job. You're kicking my family out on the street!"

"It's your choice! I'm sorry, but I have to make up the loss of money from the drop in business. I still have bills to pay too, you know!"

"I don't know how we'll survive," Mom despairs in a broken voice.

You can cut the tension with a knife as the sheriff speaks up, "Listen, I know Dorris is a great seamstress." Looking at Al, he asks, "Don't you own the laundry down the street?"

"Yeah! So?"

"Could you use a seamstress? A lot of people in the area know she's skilled in that, and it may help you both."

Al shakes his head, "I don't know. I guess we may be able to work something out, but no more charity."

"Look here, Mr. Big Man," Dorris says, "I've never asked for any charity. In fact, I've refused it. I can't help it if your grifters bled you," she replies, visibly upset over the insinuation.

The sheriff interrupts, "Look, you two. Let's just stick with the issues at hand."

Al wants this to be over, so he interjects, "Okay, I meant no harm. If you want to work for me, we'll work something out."

"Like what?"

"You work for me, and I'll pay you $5 a week and lower your rent to $15 a month."

The sheriff quickly jumps in, "That sounds pretty reasonable to me, Dorris."

"Lower my rent? I'm only paying $10 now. You're raising it by 50 percent."

Al's now upset, "You should be paying $20! You've lived there rent-free for six months! Oh, I'm sorry, for $10. Dorris, I can't go any lower than $15."

Too Old, Too Fast

"Mr. Al, I don't like it and I don't think I can make it, but I'll try."

The sheriff quickly throws in, "Then it's a deal?"

"Yeah, it's a deal," both agree.

After they stand and shake hands, Dorris heads home and runs "the deal" through her mind. She knows this may work for a while, but not for very long. It'll only be a matter of time before she'll have to do the unthinkable. Actually, she doesn't even want to consider it and tries to erase it from her mind.

The Livingstons have been struggling, too, and have lost a lot of property because of their financial situation. Walter's not in good health, partly because of the stress he's under constantly, and Maggie's doing all she can to cut corners. Dorris goes over a couple of times a week to help them out. Clyde's over there as much as he can, either helping them or taking care of Warrior, usually both. He now rides all over the place and enjoys the companionship of his horse. It's his way of dealing with the loss of his dad.

He regularly puts his arms around Warrior's neck, gives him a squeeze, and tells him, "I don't know what I would do without ya." It always brings a tear to his eye when he thinks about Dad. He remembers getting Dad's famous "bear" hugs, and the smell of the leather in that old hat. Whenever he went by the old place, he'd jump up and try to tap that old horseshoe, but, as Dad would say, "You're still too short in the britches." Harold's always around to help and give advice; he's become like Clyde's big brother.

***

Pastor Red's family has seen the same hard times as other families in the area. The garden that he and his family lived off of has dried up because of the drought. His wife contracted tuberculosis and passed away a while back, and Red hasn't been the same since. The fire's gone from his sermons, and they're not very good anymore. Clyde thinks that if Red's one of God's children, this God of his sure doesn't take very good care of him.

Time quickly passes and within a few months Dorris realizes this "deal" isn't going to work. They're back to the place where they can't buy food, fuel for the motor vehicle and other essentials. Al keeps after Mom to let Ruthie come back to work, and Mom continues to refuse. There are just too many mouths to feed, and she can't do it any longer. A decision needs to be made for the good of the whole family, and Mom knows what that means.

Late one afternoon, when the kids are out helping around the place, Mom sits down and cries. She can't believe it's come to this, but she has no choice. Knowing Clyde will be the first one home, she decides this will be the perfect time to talk with him. It's not long before she hears the sound of Clyde's cowboy boots hitting the front porch, as usual, on a dead run. Once he bounces through the front door he can sense something's wrong, and thinks, *I haven't seen Mom home from work this early before*

He says, "Hey, Mom, didn't expect to see you here so early! What's up?"

"Hi, Clyde, work is slow, and they've cut my hours and pay."

"Oh, wow, that's too bad."

"Clyde, we need to talk."

With excitement in his voice, he says, "Sure, Mom! Let's talk, just you and me."

Mom begins, "Clyde, you know how much I love you, right?"

"Sure, Mom!" Clyde replies with a puzzled look.

"Well then, what I'm about to say has nothing to do with you, our family, or me, okay?"

Now Clyde's really confused. "Sure, I guess, Mom. What cha trying to say?"

"Clyde, you know we haven't had much to eat over the past few months, right?"

"Yeah, but its okay Mom. Things'll get better."

"Clyde, it's only going to get harder. Son, you're the man of the house, and you can provide for yourself. The girls can't, unless they do what Ruthie was doing."

"Yeah, I know, Mom, and we don't want her doing that . . . right?"

"That's right, Clyde, and that's why I have to ask you to leave."

"What cha mean, *leave*?"

"Clyde, I know you're only eleven, but you've been working for a while now. The family's going to have to move into a smaller place that we can afford. Having a young man around with growing girls won't work, and we barely have enough food for the girls."

"Ya mean ya don't want me to come home anymore?"

"It's not what I want; it's what I must do. You'll find yourself a new home and begin a new life."

"Mom, what should we tell the girls?"

"Clyde, I'll tell the girls. I think it's best if you leave before they get home."

Clyde begins to cry, "Mom, I'm scared."

"I know, my son, but God will watch over you. I've packed your stuff in this bag with a little food. I love you, Son, and I always will." With that, Mom can no longer hold in her emotions. She weeps and walks into the back room. Clyde stands in the middle of the room and cries while his mind races. The room seems gray and it's hard to focus. *What just happened? Will that be the last time I ever see Mom? Where will I go, what will I do?* he wonders.

Clyde picks up his bag and bedroll and heads out the door. He walks down the road, hoping Mom will come running after him, but soon realizes it's not going to happen. Then it hits him, *This isn't the end, it's the beginning; but the beginning of what? What's going on? First I lose my dad, and now my mom and sisters, too?* Clyde's not sure what to do, so he talks to himself, "Which way do I go? Where do I go? If God's watching over me, then I don't need Him. I know you're there, God, but for some reason You don't like me, and that's fine with me. Mom said God's going to watch after me? Yeah, just like He did my dad and Red's wife. I don't need You watching out after me. I can do this myself. Fine, if this is the way it's going to be, I'll show them. I'll show everyone!"

***

Mom sits on the bed in the back room and can't believe what she just did. There are so many thoughts filling her head: *What kind of a mother am I? Putting out my young son! How'd we get to this point? Should I have tried something else? But what else is there? We never should've left the Livingstons'. I'm just too stubborn and prideful! Should I run out and stop him? No, that won't help. I just have to pull myself together before the girls come home. I sure wish Elmer was here.*

Clyde makes his way out of town and tries to think of places where he can go. He has to decide soon, or he'll be walking around in the dark. First, he thinks of going to town, but everyone knows him there. They'd wonder what he was doing and ask a bunch of questions that he doesn't want to answer. So he decides to head over to see Warrior, the only family he has now. "I can stay in the barn with 'im, but I'll sneak in so no one will know."

Walking west in the direction of the Livingstons', he notices the sun begin it's descent below the horizon. He stops and stares at it and thinks, *This is my first sunset on my own. That's one huge ball, all red and orange and the clouds look like a soft, fluffy bed to crawl into. The pink reminds me of my sisters. I'm sure going to miss them! The blue sky is the same color I remember Dad's eyes being. Dad, I wish you were here.*

He reaches the Livingstons' as the sun settles below the horizon. With dim lights coming from the house, it looks as though everyone's settled in for the evening. He'd love to go by the old place, but doesn't want anyone to see him, so he walks to the back of the barn and straight to Warrior. His horse responds with a little neigh as he wraps his arms around his neck and says, "Hello, Boy, I feel better now." His eyes start to water and he turns his back to Warrior, as if he doesn't want him to see him cry. It doesn't take long for Warrior to respond the way he normally does, even when Clyde turns his back. Warrior places his nose in the middle of his back and gives him a gentle nudge, just enough to get his attention. Clyde turns around with a big smile and, once again, hugs his beloved horse.

***

Mom walks out on the porch, sits in Elmer's old rocker and rocks back and forth. As the sun slowly sets, Mom gazes into the western sky, mesmerized at the beautiful picture it paints. The sun's like a ball of fire, while the clouds look like cotton balls in front of a pink and blue backdrop. What a beautiful scene to end such a horrible day.

Chapter 21

Harold and Clyde

It's early morning and the family begins to stir while Mom prepares breakfast. Sara runs out of the bedroom like someone's chasing her. "Mom! Mom, where are ya?" she hollers, panicked.

"I'm right here. What's wrong?"

"I went looking for Clyde, Mom, and he ain't here! Where is he?"

"That's funny. You can't find him?"

"No! What are we goin' to do?"

"Don't worry; I'm sure he's fine."

"How do ya know he's fine?"

"Oh, just a mother's instinct, I guess."

Ruthie walks out holding Rachel and rubbing her eyes, "What's all the commotion?" she inquires.

Sara nervously replies, "Clyde's gone, and we don't know where he is."

"Is that true, Mom?" Ruthie asks.

"Yeah, but I'm sure he's fine."

***

Clyde's sound asleep on a haystack inside the Livingstons' barn. Warrior walks up behind him, leans over the stall and

185

nudges him in the middle of the back. Rolling over, Clyde says, "Morning, big guy." Lying on his back, he hopes this is all one bad dream, but unfortunately it isn't. With his stomach churning, he wonders where breakfast is coming from, and then thinks, *Who's going to hire a young kid*? He hears someone walk into the barn and rolls off the hay behind a bale. Propping himself up on his elbows, he peeks around the bale to see who's there. It's Harold, and he's carrying something. Harold glances around the barn as if he's looking for something, and then walks toward Clyde. The closer he gets, the more nervous Clyde becomes. He doesn't want to scare Harold, so he quickly thinks to clear his throat, stopping Harold in his tracks. He hollers, "Who's there?"

"Harold, it's me, Clyde," he answers as he stands up.

"Clyde! What cha doin' here this early?"

"Well, to tell ya the truth, I slept here."

"What? Why'd ya do that?"

Looking down, trying to hold back his emotions, Clyde explains the events of the previous day. He looks up at Harold and explains, "I didn't know where else to go." He can't hold back any longer, and tears stream down his face.

Regaining his composure, he looks up at Harold and asks, "What cha doin' with the bag?"

"Well, I have a little story myself," he tells Clyde. "Last night the Livingstons had me over for dinner. Afterwards we talked, and they explained that they had to let me go. They were so apologetic, I felt bad for them, Clyde! They're going through such tough times that their resources have evaporated too, and they may not even be able to hang on to the ranch. They paid me, even gave me a bonus to help till I get another job. I've decided to head east to look for work."

Clyde eagerly asks, "Can I come with ya?"

"I don't know, Clyde. It might be best for ya to stay here. Ya know, just in case something happens and ya can go back home."

Clyde responds hopefully, "Harold, ya told me your story, how the same thing happened to you when you were twelve.

I'm almost eleven and I'm a hard worker. We can put our money together and help each other."

"Well, I've always thought of you as my little brother. Why not; it might be fun?"

"Can we take Warrior?"

"Sorry, we've got no way to haul 'im."

"I'll ride him!" Clyde says.

Shaking his head, Harold responds, "Clyde, that's nonsense. A horse can only travel about twenty miles a day and costs a lot to care for. Put that foolish idea behind ya, and start thinking like a man."

"Oh, okay, but I'm sure gonna miss my horse." Once again Clyde tears up, but quickly pulls himself together. Harold places his arm on Clyde's shoulder and softly answers, "Time to grow up!"

***

After a lot of conversation, Mom convinces the girls that Clyde's all right. They go about their chores and get ready for school without any further questioning. Mom thinks, *This is going to be a tough day, not knowing where Clyde is.* With only enough food for the girls, she prepares their lunches. The girls, meanwhile, get Rachel ready to take to work with Mom.

***

Harold pulls up his 1928 Model A roadster pick-up truck. It's nothing to look at, but whose vehicle in this area is? Harold had purchased it from a rancher in Texas who had bought another one, and knowing Harold's story, sold it to him for a song. The truck has an enclosed cab with an open bed. It doesn't take long for Clyde to pack; he simply throws his bag and bedroll in the back. Harold, on the other hand, has quite a bit, so Clyde jumps right in and gives Harold a hand loading his stuff. Once loaded, they pull out of the driveway and head to town.

Too Old, Too Fast

As they drive along, Harold asks Clyde, "Ya sure ya want to do this, Half-pint? I've got to stop in town for fuel, and ya can stay there if ya want." Without hesitating Clyde responds, "Not much to stay there for; I'm with ya all the way."

"Okay! But just know it's not going to be easy."

"Yeah, I guess."

***

As the girls leave for school, Sara asks, "Mom, can I go looking for Clyde?"

She angrily replies, "No! You need to get to school, and I need to get to work. I've already told you he's fine. We'll probably see him tonight!" Mom struggles, knowing she's lying to the girls, but she tries to convince herself that this is the right thing to do. Her thinking is that, *Telling them the truth will only make them feel guilty, too.*

Ruthie kindly requests, "Mom, if he's not home tonight, can Sara and I go asking around?"

Mom, tired of the questions, firmly says, "Girls, we'll deal with that tonight! Get to school!"

It's a short walk to school for Sara and Ruthie, and they talk about Clyde as they go.

"This doesn't make sense!" Sara proclaims. She has an inquisitive mind and thinks everything that happens is suspicious. The scary part is that she's right most of the time.

"What do you mean, 'it doesn't make sense'?" Ruthie questions.

"Why doesn't Mom want to know where Clyde was last night, or this morning, unless she already knows?"

"You think Mom's lying to us?" Ruthie asks.

"No, I don't think so; well maybe. I don't know. What do you think?"

"I don't remember Mom ever lying to us, do you?" Sara shakes her head as Ruthie continues. "Why would she do that? It doesn't make sense."

"Me neither. Let's wait an' see what happens tonight."

C. E. Andrews

As they're talking, Sara notices a truck coming down the road. She hollers at Ruthie, "Watch out! Don't cross the street; here comes a motor vehicle."

***

While in town Harold stops for petrol. A familiar face walks out the station door and greets Harold with, "Fill 'er up?"

"Sure," Harold replies.

After placing the gas nozzle in the filler tube, he walks over to wash the window and acknowledges Clyde, "Hey there, Clyde," he looks up and nods. As he sits there, he notices things he's never paid much attention to before. He can't recall ever seeing the glass cylinders at the top of the pump with the light reddish gasoline inside. The sign on top of the pumps reads, "Conoco." Clyde looks at the town through new eyes; it's the same old town, but he views it from a different perspective this morning. He observes the Main Street stores. Even though he's been in them before, they don't look the same. The school's down the block on the right. Sitting there, he thinks, *I'm sure going to miss this place!* Blinking his eyes as if to wake himself up, he hears the attendant ask Harold, "See ya loaded up there in the back. Ya leavin' town?"

"Yeah, not much work 'round here anymore," Harold replies.

"Where ya headed?"

"East and then south into Oklahoma or Texas. We'll stop when we find work."

"Well, good luck to ya both."

"Thanks! May see ya again one day," Harold answers.

Clyde's never thought about the prices of things before, but the sign above the pump jumps out at him: seventeen cents a gallon.

Wow, it took $1.20 to fill the tank, Clyde thinks. *I couldn't pay for that!* This launches him into second-guessing his decision. *How will we ever make it?*

Harold starts the truck and pulls away from the pumps as Clyde looks down the street and sees Sara walking to school with Ruthie. Sara grabs Ruthie's arm to keep her from walking in front of the truck. As they drive by, he thinks, *What do I do? Should I wave? Should I ignore 'em*? By the time he thinks it through, it's too late. Slouching down and putting his head back, he closes his eyes and thinks, *That may be the last time I ever see my sisters.* Turning his head so Harold doesn't see, tears well up in his eyes. Gazing out the window, he reflects back over the last two years. *Since Dad died, it's been so hard; things just always seem to go wrong. Ruthie and Jonathan, Mom asking me to leave, leaving Warrior, and now I may never see my sisters again. What else can go wrong? Boy, if God is really there, He must really hate me.*

Sara looks at Ruthie, "Did you see who was in that truck?"

"Not sure, who'd you see?"

"Looked like Clyde!"

"Yeah, that's what I thought, too."

"Wonder where he's goin'?"

"Probably just riding out to Goldberg's for something."

"Yeah, well, at least we know he's okay."

As they pass by the service station, the attendant is at the pumps with another car. He's got a crush on Ruthie, and as they walk by, he hollers, "Hey Ruthie!" This gets Sara mad, and she thinks, *Guys always say 'hi' to her and ignore me. What am I, chopped liver?* She's already worked up, so this time she hollers, "What, ya don't see me?"

"Oh, yeah, sorry small fry. Hey to you, too. Just saw your little brother!"

"Yeah, we saw 'im too in that motor vehicle with Harold, right?" Sara responds.

"Yep, that's it. With Harold, who used to work for the Livingstons."

"Used to?"

"Yep, they had to let him go."

"Wow! Wonder what Clyde's doing with him?"

He looks up from washing the windshield and replies, "Said they're headin' east to Oklahoma or Texas—something like that."

"What?" Ruthie screams, "He took my little brother with him?"

"Looks that way to me," the attendant answers.

"Come on, Sara! We have to get home and tell Mom!"

As the girls hurry off, the attendant hollers, "Ruthie, wanna have a soda later?"

Ruthie shakes her head and waves her arm to let him know she has more important things to take care of. He walks back into the office, thinking, *Probably wasn't a good time to ask!*

Ruthie and Sara run about halfway home before they realize that Mom's at work. They turn around and sprint to the cleaners, bursting through the front door. Mom's in the back working on a dress.

"Mom! Mom!" Ruthie shouts.

"I'm right here! Why aren't you two in school?" Mom demands.

"Mom, we just saw Clyde in a truck with Harold!" Sara injects.

"Oh, no big deal, over the past few months they've gotten pretty close. They're just going somewhere together."

"No, Mom! We talked to the station attendant and he said,'they filled up and told him they're headed to Oklahoma or something!'" Ruthie exclaims.

"What? I don't believe it." Mom replies.

"Should we call the police and stop 'em?" Sara asks.

Mom doesn't know what to say. She sits there with a puzzled look, searching for just the right words. "Let's not panic. If that's what Clyde wants, we need to allow him the freedom to do it."

This takes the girls by surprise. They look at each other and can't believe what Mom's saying. "What?" Ruthie jumps in, "Just let him go? Mom, he's only eleven! How will he survive?"

"Now listen up! You know how we've been struggling; he may have seen that and decided to leave. This may be good for everyone."

Sara stands there with her mouth open. She questions, "Just let 'im go? Allow him the freedom? Ya didn't do that for Ruthie!

Ya went after her!" As soon as she got it out of her mouth, she knew she was in trouble.

"Listen to me, young lady, I'm still the mom, and don't you forget it. You had better get to school if you know what's good for you." Tears stream down Sara's cheeks as she and Ruthie walk out of the cleaners.

Ruthie looks at Sara and asks, "What just happened?"

"I don't know. How can she just let Clyde go? You know, Clyde's leaving is all my fault!"

"What? How can you say that?" Ruthie asks.

"Well, remember when Clyde and I got into trouble and he ratted me out?"

"Yeah, so what?"

Well, I told him I'd never talk to him again." Now weeping, she says, "I didn't mean it! I didn't want him to leave. Ruthie, I'm so sorry I made Clyde leave."

"You didn't make him leave; no one did. He did it all on his own, and I'm really mad that he deserted us. I'll never forgive him. The biggest question is; why doesn't Mom want to go after him?"

★★★

The microwave buzzer goes off and Grandma hollers, "Enough storytelling for now; dinner's ready." The kids let out a moan and say, "Not now, Grandpa's not done yet. We want to know what happens to Great Grandpa."

As I lift my grandson to carry him to the table, one of the grandkids asks, "What about the hat and horseshoe, Grandpa?"

"We'll get to that after dinner. Now you kids listen to your grandma. Off to the bathroom, clean up, and then get to the table."